SECLUSION POINT

SECLUSION POINT

A NOVEL

RENEGADE SPIRIT: BOOK THREE

JERRY B. JENKINS
& JOHN PERRODIN

THOMAS NELSON
Since 1798

NASHVILLE DALLAS MEXICO CITY RIO DE JANEIRO BEIJING

Published in Nashville, Tennessee, by Thomas Nelson. Thomas Nelson is a registered trademark of Thomas Nelson, Inc.

Thomas Nelson, Inc. titles may be purchased in bulk for educational, business, fund-raising, or sales promotional use. For information, please e-mail SpecialMarkets@ThomasNelson.com.

Library of Congress Cataloging-in-Publication Data has been applied for.

ISBN 978-1-59554-401-8

Printed in the United States of America
08 09 10 11 QW 9 8 7 6 5 4 3 2

Thank you, Jesus, for your boundless
grace and enduring love.

—John Perrodin

Acknowledgments

Many thanks to Michelle Cox for helping me juggle multiple book projects. Your friendship and writing skill are blessings from God.

I also wish to express sincere appreciation to Leslie Peterson for her editorial acumen. You helped make this volume a thrilling finale to the Renegade Spirit Series.

And finally, thank you to my wife, Sue. I love you. Always have, always will.

—John Perrodin

In *The Tattooed Rats*, Patch Johnson stood alone—one faithful young man against a high school full of unbelievers. Though scorned, he wasn't afraid to tell others about Jesus. In *Demon's Bluff*, Patch and his friends moved an entire town to battle a demonic horde threatening to take over. He discovered that prayer changes lives, starting with his own. Finally, in *Seclusion Point*, Patch is alone again, chased by Cheryl McCry and wondering what God wants to teach him next.

The Kids

Patrick "Patch" Johnson: Wants life to get back to normal—whatever that means. He settles in a small town and puts prayer to the test.

Erin: Has caught the bug called "Christianity," but doesn't mind too much. Her only problems are figuring out who can be trusted with her secret, and how to help someone special.

Molly: No one had better tell her to keep *her* faith quiet. She's ready to face anything for Jesus, and nobody—not even McCry—scares her.

Granger: A basketball player with a special ring that allows him to see into hearts—even his own. He and Nancy used to be close.

Marty: The class World Peace Alliance (WPA) representative. His only goal is to capture Christians and work his way up in the organization.

Claudia: Formerly "The Claw." She loves God but isn't sure it's smart to be too open about the truth.

Barry and Hope: Friends of Trevor, the demon who made life miserable for Patch. They've come for revenge.

Nancy: She's changed since her encounters at Demon's Bluff, but she can't decide if it's really safe to serve God. And if it's right to let her heart make decisions for her.

Jarrod: Patch's new friend from Demon's Bluff. He helped map Patch's path when he escaped the WPA.

The Adults

Cheryl McCry: A powerful force in the World Peace Alliance one-world regulatory system, she's committed to the extermination of Christians.

Ma and Pa Stone: Formerly famous gospel singers, the Stones believe they know what God's will is for Patch.

1

CHERYL MCCRY WAS back in black.

A few months earlier her boss, Frazier, had hired a brain-dead consultant. Someone who'd decided McCry needed a makeover demanded McCry become a softer, gentler head enforcer for the World Peace Alliance. Despite her objections, McCry was forced to wear bright jungle greens and a new hairstyle.

She'd hated every minute of it. Hated tripping over high heels and cracking off painted nails. Her world was guns and explosive devices, not spin doctors selling baloney. But Frazier refused to hear her complaints and diligently tried to remake McCry in her own slick image. It never quite worked.

But Frazier had kept at it until the day she died.

McCry dipped her head as she plodded past the open casket. Poor Frazier. Still quite an eyeful, especially wearing full makeup, her hair done up in a silver tiara. A beautiful woman, her boss. Now she was a gorgeous corpse.

As McCry made her way to a seat in the back, a thought tickled her: no one had discovered the cause of death. Strange, really, especially since McCry herself had headed up the investigation. She smirked.

Maybe she knew something about it, maybe she didn't. All that mattered was that she had used the opportunity to snatch more power within the WPA organization. With Frazier out of the way, McCry could get back to business. Do things the way she wanted.

After Demon's Bluff, she had scores to settle. Patrick Johnson would not be allowed to humiliate her and remain free. He had to be caught and punished. Summer was done and school was about to start. Patch's friends would be ready to hit the books, trying desperately to blend in.

The Tattooed Rats, a loosely strung group of Christ-Kids and adults, had caused her no end of problems. Time for her to fumigate that nest of believers.

The man at the podium, the chief officer of the WPA, eulogized Frazier's life. Telling lies about her gentle manner, her winning ways. Truth was, everyone had hated the woman. She only got her way because of her looks, which was something McCry had never thought fair.

Oh well. Now Frazier rested in a standard-issue casket.

Funerals never depressed McCry; she thought of the positives. More air, food, and water for her. And one less creep to contend with.

The boring speaker turned the podium over to another. This could take all morning. McCry popped open her electronic notebook and starting jotting notes.

Increase reward program. Encourage more betrayals. Double the credits for a Christian. Turn in one, get double the store voucher. Turn in two and get triple.

Inspirational. She silently thanked her former boss for this time of reflection.

PATCH MISSED THE Tat Rats. How was a guy supposed to survive without a gang to hang around with? Maybe he should've taken Jarrod up on his offer. This going-it-alone thing was tough.

He took the opportunity for one last call to his mentor.

"Gary here."

When he heard the voice, Patch smiled. Gary was Patch's friend, a guy he trusted. He was the one who had found him safe places in the past.

"Can I come back?" That's what Patch wanted. To stop running and get back in with the Tattooed Rats.

"No. Would like you to, but it's not possible now." Gary sounded firm.

"So what's in store for me?" Patch tried not to let Gary hear his annoyance.

"You might not like the name, but Sticklerville, Kansas, is the perfect hideout," Gary said. "No WPA presence to speak of. Lots of Christians, low key. Should be safe for you."

Patch wanted to know what *safe* meant. Certainly not the same as *free*. Probably meant hiding underground, running from house to house. He hadn't enjoyed anything like a family life until he lived with Jarrod in Demon's Bluff. The guy was like a brother; his parents cared about him almost as much as his own did.

Had. *May Mom and Dad rest in peace.*

"I trust you." That was all he could think to say. He didn't want to do this, but he had no choice. He assumed Gary had good reasons for directing him to Sticklerville.

"Got a great family set up for you. Believe it or not, there's actually a list of folks trying to serve as foster parents. You're kind of a celebrity."

Patch heard the TV blaring in the background. It was one of the ways the Tat Rats kept informed. Watching the screen, finding out where the hot zones were and steering clear.

"I'm ready." Patch wasn't, but he was trying to get himself psyched. "You sure they're okay?"

"We ran the computer check twice. Came up clean. They're minor stars. They sing at underground worship concerts. Years ago they were huge on the singing circuit. Might even have heard of them: Mama and Papa Stone."

Heard of them? His parents had been raving groupies once upon a time. They loved the old-time sound, backed up with lots of hand-crafted instruments. Not Patch's taste, but he didn't mind hearing them as background music.

"Give me the details."

Gary talked fast as Patch took notes. On to a new adventure. He was sure things would go fine. After all, he trusted his Tat Rat brothers and sisters.

AFTER THE CALL to Gary and farewells to Jarrod and his parents, Patch started walking. At the edge of town he passed a telephone pole. A tattered paper hung there, and he yanked it off. Rusted staples still stuck to the edge. His thin face stared back at him. He was plastered all over thousands of the cheap WANTED posters.

The next town wasn't far, but someone—anyone—could turn him in before he got there. All they had to do was contact the World Peace Alliance to claim the reward. Patch knew Cheryl McCry waited for the call that would lead her to him.

Patch stared at his image on the poster, framed in black. Would anyone recognize him? Over the summer he'd gotten thinner, taller. His hair was longer and he'd let a first-fuzz goatee grow. Didn't provide much coverage, but any disguise was better than none.

He sighed. He was lonely. Even though he knew it was right, he was sad Jarrod was staying behind in Demon's Bluff. His friend had jammed Patch's backpack with some extra hidden cash. Nearly fifty dollars. Patch pictured his brother in Christ cleaning out his closet to find this much. If Patch had known, he might have snagged a bus ride. Course, then the money would be gone already.

Jarrod had also snuck in a pay-as-you-go cell phone. What a

gift, especially since it was already loaded with several hundred minutes of talk time.

When he'd found the stash, he'd wanted to go back and thank Jarrod, but one glimpse of him and Patch would've found it even tougher to leave. He and his parents had offered Patch a home, a family. But he couldn't put them in such danger.

Patch would take a train when he got to the next town. After he'd talked with Gary, he and Jarrod had scoped out a route. North from central Nevada to the next state, and then to the place called Sticklerville, Kansas. Soon as he arrived, he'd have to start blending in. Get involved in school, keep a low profile. That was his life now that McCry had him in her sights.

And there were the demons, too. Trevor might have disappeared, but his demons-in-training, Barry and Hope, still knew Patch's name. And he figured they wouldn't give up on finding him any more than McCry would.

He was desperate to become invisible. Fast.

Kansas okay with you, God?

As he walked along the shoulder of the road, Patch cracked open his journal. He halted a moment to read: *Where to now, God? I want your path. You smashed the teeth of demons and saved me. So where to next?*

He jammed the book in the backpack and prayed, clearing his mind of worries and clinging to some promises. The road was long. Heat bounced back from the blacktop.

A car slowed and a man leaned out the window, asking Patch if he wanted a ride. Patch kept his head down and declined. He'd learned it was better to keep to himself, even if his feet were sore.

The man tipped his baseball cap and drove on. Patch watched until the vehicle slowly shrunk to the size of a red toy and disappeared, then trudged toward the setting sun. He'd reach the next town in time to grab a bite and check the train schedule.

A quiet life hidden under a Kansas rainbow. That would work.

2

CLAUDIA COULDN'T BELIEVE she was back in her own living room. She wasn't the same girl who'd left several days before. Demon's Bluff had shifted her thinking forever.

"I'm a Christian," she said, practicing the words aloud. "A Christ-Kid."

"Impossible!" Her mom came into the room. Claudia had already told her about the incredible change in her life. The woman hadn't taken it well. Now she pointed a long finger. "I won't have it. You've caused me enough trouble over the years."

Claudia had heard the speech before—about how difficult it was to raise a girl like her, all alone.

"But Mom, God has changed my heart. I'm different."

"Still seem selfish to me."

"Sorry, Mom." Claudia reached for her mother's hand, but the woman yanked away and slumped into a rocker.

Claudia wondered how Erin and the others were doing. They were all home, too, but nothing felt the same. Even with school almost about to start, things felt strange, up in the air. Claudia silently prayed for Nancy, Molly, Granger, Patch, Erin, and her new friend, Jarrod.

Her mother had been watching her. "Maybe something *is* different about you," she said. "Otherwise you'd still be arguing."

Claudia wanted to retort with a, "That's what I mean." But she couldn't. She shouldn't. Something had changed inside, and it had worked its way from her heart to her mouth.

Amazing.

GRANGER KNEW MARTY had come up behind him. He also knew what his old friend was getting ready to say. That's because he had the ultimate tool: a tell-all ring that worked like a genie in a bottle. All he had to do was ask.

"I'm not the one you're looking for," Granger said. "They are."

He didn't have to turn around to know that Marty was wondering how he'd known. "Huh?" Granger heard him grunt.

Granger's mind-reading trick boggled the brain. That's what he loved about it. He could hear Marty's thoughts as if he were listening to a book on tape. And he could tell Marty was baffled at how Granger knew what he was thinking.

It's easy. If you have the right tool, Granger thought. *And I do.* He spread the fingers of his right hand, looked at the impressive silver ring. Priceless. And scuffed. Probably from when he'd rolled around in the desert, kicking demon tails. But with it he could do things no one else could.

Enough tormenting. Granger faced his friend. He wasn't sure if he was glad—or afraid—to have him back in town. At least he had the ring to keep Marty under control.

"What are you talking about?" Marty said. His hair flamed like a ripe apple. He'd buzzed it regulation short. WPA camp had packed bulging muscle onto his frame. His shoulders were huge. Granger felt scrawny by comparison, until he remembered that he was the one with the ring.

"I read minds, okay?" Granger pumped Marty's hand. No sense getting on the big guy's bad side. "Look, I'm not trying to freak you out. Just wanted to let you know. Figured with my help you might want to earn some extra credit." He jabbed Marty with an elbow. "You know? Get in good with your instructors at WPA."

Marty's face showed surprise. Then utter confusion. Then indifference. Marty wasn't the flashiest tie on the rack. "Missed hanging out with you last summer," he said. His chin jutted, clean shaven.

"Course you did," Granger said. "My break was wild. Demon's Bluff Spirit Fest was an event to die for."

Pictures came into his mind. Granger wondered how much he could tell his friend. The eternal question: could he trust him? Toughest thing was that Granger wasn't sure he even wanted to help Marty. They'd had their differences in the past. The guy wasn't exactly the picture of stability.

But he could use him to show off with the ring.

What good was having a super power if no one else knew?

"Some of the old gang got religion," Granger said.

There, it was out.

Marty perked up. *This could help me with officer placement.*

Granger heard the thought loud and clear. So predictable, so self-centered, so Marty. Clearly the guy was one of them now. A WPA convert to the core. Gung ho to capture his first Christian. So what if the people he'd turn over used to be his best friends?

But that's what made Granger so valuable. Someone with direct access to the other world—the place where secrets were kept. Granger loved tapping in, finding out who was cheating, who was lying, and who was pretending. The feeling it gave him was better than the high he got raising dust on the track.

"Who you talking about?" Marty pretended disinterest. But Granger knew better. Marty's thoughts zoomed ahead to rewards, promotions, travel.

Granger eavesdropped with a grin. *Keeping the ring was a good move.* He'd been looking forward to school, reading the teachers' minds and driving his parents crazy. Grades never mattered that much to him; he had his sports. But the idea of being the top academic kid, rolling over the ones who deserved the title, did something for him. He'd gotten a kick out of it: head of the class without even trying. Awesome.

But this latest feature, the ability to turn in or protect a friend . . . Wow, that was real power.

For the first time Granger was excited for school to start. He hadn't felt that way since kindergarten, when he'd gotten to pick out new crayons.

3

EVEN IN THE Demon Zone, time marched on. Of course, Trevor was gone. Slashed to smithereens by the swords of the enemy. Hope and Barry would never again benefit from their mentor's clawing comments. The only thing they could do was keep him alive in their memories. Nurse their grudges, keep them warm and curdled.

Hope realized demons never built monuments to their fallen. They spit on the graves of the defeated. And after an encounter with an angel, there wasn't enough left to bury. A wisp of smoke, that wretched smell. Bye-bye Trevor.

It was Graduation Day. Flabbygums, their ancient teacher, stood at the front of the group, his bow tie askew. He looked miserable in the twisted robe, one arm in, the other out. While he droned on about their accomplishments and future, Hope's thoughts flitted back to the creature who'd given them their start in the human harassment biz. Would have been nice to hear Trevor jeer, slap his tail, and stomp his feet as she and Barry walked the aisle, got their wrinkled certificates.

Wherever would Hope put hers? It's not like demons had offices where they could hang framed awards. The whole thing seemed stupid to her, but it was tradition. So what could she say?

She and Barry were being released to pursue their assignments. And that was what she was waiting for. Of course she already knew who she'd be chasing; Flabbygums had already promised them Patrick Johnson. Patch. A pathetic boy who had serious problems picking his friends.

Patrick Johnson and his herd of confused Christ-Kids were as good as dead. All of them. All she and Barry had to do was find them.

WRITING REPORTS. CHERYL McCry hated this part of her job. She liked the bottom line, not the explanations. And the bottom line was that Patrick Johnson was still at large. After Frazier's demise, she had promoted Patch to the top of her most-wanted list. She hated him that much.

Her time in the Nevada desert near Demon's Bluff had taught her that weird things happen sometimes. But she rationalized them. So what if she'd seen some buff teenager strip off his human costume and show the gnarled body beneath it? That didn't mean it was true. Demons didn't exist. Period. Even if they stood before her, she refused to believe. There had to be another explanation. Sometimes it was her job to think of one.

"Done with that yet? I need to sign off on all of them," McCry barked at her new intern, a wimp with "Marty" lettered on his nametag. He stood before her, his arms piled with papers. Tough looking on the outside, she could see by his grimace that he had a lot to learn. With less than a week until school started, she was working him in. He was lucky. He hadn't seen her bad mood yet. He was hers to torment every afternoon through the semester. She was just getting started a little early.

Not that he wouldn't get something out of it too. It was the age-old pattern: he'd do her grunt work now for a promised officer position later. If he graduated.

"Look," McCry said, "that Patch kid's still running, and you know how I feel about loose ends." She picked up a letter opener and jabbed it into her desk blotter.

"Patch Johnson is officially gone," Marty said. His voice cracked.

"Speak up, soldier."

"Missing and presumed dead."

McCry nodded. Fine. Maybe she could use this mumble-mouthed slacker. "See what your friends say. Go undercover."

Marty fell all over himself agreeing, catching papers as they slipped, then scurried from the room.

McCry sat back in her chair. Could be the grunt would return with something useable. Though she doubted it.

No matter. She was certain she would see Patch again.

She'd make sure of it.

STICKLERVILLE, KANSAS, HAD a ring to it. Big enough to disappear in, but small enough to get around on foot. That's what Jarrod said when they searched online. Patch bought his ticket, then gorged on scrambled eggs, sausage, catsup, and crackers before boarding.

As the train slowly moved east and the rocky landscape outside his window changed to green fields, Patch got out his journal and scribbled his summer story. Mostly he wrote about Erin. He couldn't stop thinking about her, about her smile, her brown eyes flecked with green, her freckles. Something had changed between them. Maybe it was when they'd raced after the dinosaur-sized demon together. Maybe it had happened during their private talks. Patch couldn't put his finger on the exact moment he'd realized she was more than a friend.

But he knew she was. That's why he'd scraped together some money to buy her something special.

He pulled the ring out of his pocket and stared at it. A circle that meant friendship. He wondered if he'd ever be able to give it to her.

If he'd be allowed to thank her for standing with him at Demon's Bluff.

He could still feel their good-bye kiss.

Too bad he felt this way about her, because he imagined he would never see her again. Could never see her again. Not in person. It wouldn't be safe. And one thing he'd never ever do again was put his friends in danger.

THE SHINING ONE saluted. His duty was to obey. Come lightning or earthquake, hurricane or drought, he would go where he was directed. Help as he was told.

He stood his ground waiting for the order.

"Watch Patrick Johnson. I have enormous plans for his future," the Commander said. "He will suffer a time of testing. As every human must."

"Will intervention be permitted, sir?" The Shining One was a stickler for details. He would not move a fingertip unless he'd been given appropriate clearance. Eons of experience had shown him that the Commander's judgments were always fair, always true. Though sometimes they seemed logical only after the fact.

His was not to reason and pry. That lesson he'd learned well.

"You will watch him, pray with him, keep me informed. And take the next step only when the command is given."

"Of course, sir." The angel kneeled. When he tipped his head back and opened his eyes, the Commander was gone.

4

As Little Brothers go, Terry was the cutest. So why couldn't Erin get Patch's crooked grin out of her mind?

Back home from Demon's Bluff, school started in less than five days. But nothing seemed the same. One day she'd been battling the forces of evil in Nevada, the next she was fussing because her parents wouldn't let her use the car.

Having a wiggly brother around helped distract her.

"Come here. Let me have a look at that lizard again." She couldn't believe what she was saying.

"He's the best, isn't he?" Terry said, holding it in cupped hands.

"He certainly is reptilian."

The lizard stuck his tongue out, and she scratched him under the neck.

"You can borrow him, if you want," Terry said.

Their mom appeared at the door, dressed like a queen. "Put that beast back in its box."

"I need to pick up school supplies," Erin said. She wanted the car keys bad.

Mrs. Morgan smiled. Never a good sign. "I have some errands to run. I'll be happy to take you."

ALTHOUGH SHE'D CALMED down over the last couple of days, Claudia's mom continued to fuss about Claudia's change, which she was adamantly against.

"It's too dangerous. What will the other kids do if they find out?"

Claudia had to admit her mom made sense. With the WPA shoving antireligious views into every student's brain, telling the world she was a believer would be foolish.

For the first time Claudia felt sorry for her mom. *She looks old, and I'm the reason. I need to make things easier for her, not harder.*

"I could lose my job," her mom said. "The WPA might force us out of this home."

Claudia hadn't thought of that. "What do you want me to do?"

Her mom pushed gray hair out of her eyes. "We all go through phases. It's normal. Just keep yours quiet for now."

"And it'll go away?" Claudia couldn't imagine that. God had saved her. He had answered her prayers.

Her mom smiled. "Exactly. Let's hope."

Claudia smiled back and let her mother think she believed her. But as soon as the woman left the room, she picked up a phone and dialed. "Hey."

"Hey, Claw," Nancy said, sounding irritated.

Claudia bit her lip. She didn't want that nickname anymore. "So, what's up? Have you talked to anyone lately?"

"Haven't seen Granger since we got back, if that's what you mean. Listen, I'm just going to say it: I know you want another shot at him, but he's my boyfriend."

"Oh, that stuff is history." How could she get Nancy to believe? Nancy couldn't read minds anymore without her ring, so they had to talk things out. "I was just wondering about the gang in general."

"Forget it, Claw—dee—ah," Nancy said.

This was not going well. "Could you at least—"

The phone clicked sharply.

Sigh. Guess she'd have to find out on her own.

Somehow she'd hoped that Christians got along better than other people. Not so far.

H OPE AND BARRY coiled up together on a rock pile reading Flabby-gums's favorite pick: *The Screwtape Letters* by C. S. Lewis. They'd graduated, sure, but Hope didn't want to stop learning, and she knew that the Lewis classic was filled with tips. Tidbits on how to abuse and manipulate the foolish pride of humans.

"I'm bored." Barry clawed at the book cover.

"Then your brain's going to rot," Hope said.

"Why do we have to study stuff that's so old?" Barry tore out a page, crumpled it, his breath crisping the paper into a fireball. "I have my own ideas about tormenting these creatures."

Hope shifted on the mound to get more comfortable. "Don't read, then." She held out her hand for his copy. "Must be nice to know everything already."

"It is," Barry said.

He was sounding more like Trevor every day.

Hope watched as he took off into the sky, wings churning the still air. She wouldn't let him distract her. Mind games were among the best techniques available. Fill the human head with distracting thoughts and they'll never get around to the spiritual things. That's what Screwtape taught.

And it had worked for centuries.

Barry swooped over Hope's head, reached for her book. He thought he was sneaky. Without a backward glance, she shifted, lifted her tail into the air, and tripped him. She stole a peek at him spinning in smoky circles.

Hope remembered Flabbygums's words from class. "With the weak-minded your power is great," he said. "They try so hard to forget what they don't understand that they won't even remember having met you." Her wizened instructor taught that demon minds had an enormous advantage over the puny intellect of men and women. "They forget lessons learned. Almost instantly."

"They're that weak?" Hope had asked.

Flabbygums picked his teeth with a long bone. "Absolutely."

And we can have that much fun, Hope thought.

"Of course," Flabbygums said, reading her mind.

5

PATCH LOOKED FROM the postcard to the gazebo in the center of town. Swing sets swayed with children, moms and dads relaxed on benches under leafy trees. A big brother pulled his sister in a red wagon. Nothing like Demon's Bluff, and yet almost the same. Small-town smiles. A guy couldn't help but feel comfortable.

A couple of teen girls waved at him, then giggled at each other. He grinned and waved back.

He instantly felt at home in Sticklerville. He shouldn't have any trouble fitting in. And a small town like this would be barely a blip on the WPA's radar.

He looked around. There was a fire station with an antique hook-and-ladder truck out front, a corner drugstore, a brick-front library, and a police station.

Patch wasn't afraid of the cops here. He barged into the station, smile wide. "Good afternoon," he said to two officers playing checkers. "Just got into town." He slung his backpack at his feet. "I'm trying to find Ma and Pa Stone."

The heavier man stood and got on the phone. The taller one gave

Patch a Coke. "You couldn't have picked a better place. Or nicer people." He gave a big smile. Like he'd just won the lottery.

Man, what perkiness, Patch thought. He looked at the WANTED posters on the bulletin board. His face wasn't there. *Thank you, God.*

The pudgy officer got off the phone. "They should be pulling up any minute. Those two are always helping out unfortunates." He looked Patch up and down. "Like you."

Gary and the Tat Rats were right. The Stones had a sterling reputation. Maybe this time he'd get it right from the start.

ERIN PLANNED TO meet Claudia, Nancy, and, hopefully, Molly tonight to talk things out before school started. Erin didn't know what to do. On the one hand, Claudia was right. They couldn't go blabbing about what had happened at Demon's Bluff. No one would believe them. They'd be branded idiots.

But if Erin was a Christian, could she remain silent? If she was afraid to tell anyone what she believed, what good was she?

Of course, there was Terry to think about. She wanted to be around him for a long time. He would be the first person she told about Jesus.

Being around Terry again made Erin think about Patch's sister, Jenny. His baby sister had died in one of McCry's raids.

Erin choked up. If anyone did anything to Terry—

Her mom swept into the living room, dust rag in hand. "Company tonight."

"Anyone I know?"

Her mother gave her a strange smile. "I should say. You remember Ms. McCry, don't you?"

This could not be a joke. "But why?" was all Erin could manage.

"She has a favor to ask of us."

Erin felt sick. *What's going on?*

She told her mother she was planning to meet with Claudia and the others. She pled, she argued, she explained. No use. Her mother demanded that she stay home.

"I guarantee you that whatever Ms. McCry has to say will be far more interesting than your little get-together."

This was bad. What if someone found out? How could Erin explain having that woman in their home? Her friends would think she was a traitor.

Why in the world is McCry coming over, anyway?

A few hours later, she knew. And the answer both sickened and frightened her.

"She's alive?" she said to McCry. Her heart bashed against her rib cage as she looked from McCry to her parents. This woman had her questioning every word they had ever told her. Could she ever trust them again?

"We've known from the beginning," Mrs. Morgan said, obviously proud. Erin's father sat next to her, nodding. Terry played at their feet, revving a car between Ms. McCry's shoes.

The grown-ups stayed so calm. She wanted to act adult, too, but she was angry. "So why didn't you let her stay here?"

McCry was all business, her smile thin. "We didn't see how it could help. Besides, the little girl has done much better than Patch in foster care."

Keep the Christ-Kids separate, right? Break their hearts, one at a time.

"She was always out there, just in case," McCry said. "Maybe it's time to use her to bring Patch back."

"And you need my help," Erin said.

"We need you to take her in, take care of her," McCry said.

"There will be a reward," her mom said. "Of course we'll all share it." She gestured toward Terry.

Erin had trouble staying seated. She wanted to find Patch. Now. And tell him that his sister was alive.

THE TWO MADE quite a pair. Patch had seen their faces on countless old CDs. His parents were avid collectors. But in person the words "larger than life" took on new meaning. Both Ma and Pa Stone were too big to reach around.

"Come here, young fellow." The man, in a deep bass voice, spoke first. "I've been told that you're quite a character."

Patch felt something twitch at the back of his brain. A warning. "Good to meet you, sir."

The officers stood to the side. The thinner cop said, "Our local celebrities. You are one lucky kid."

Patch decided to look for the positive in the pair. Just because he didn't care for their music didn't mean they weren't wonderful people.

The woman wore a tropical muumuu in shades of orange, green, purple, and red. She playfully shoved her husband aside and surrounded Patch with arms like tree branches. For a moment, he wasn't sure he would survive.

"You're exactly right." She snuffled and wiped a tear with a tissue.

"Thanks for taking me in." Patch stepped back after she freed him from the bear clasp. "Everyone speaks so highly of you."

"As well they should, young feller." Pa stood beside his wife and reached a long arm around her shoulders. "This sweet thing is the best cook on the plains."

Patch didn't doubt it. "I am hungry."

"Course you are. A growing boy." Ma Stone fluttered long lashes. "Likely you'll try to eat our pantry empty." She didn't seem to be joking. In fact, Patch thought she sounded worried.

He was still picking up weird vibes, but they seemed harmless enough. He looked forward to some good food and plenty of it. And on Monday school started; he wanted to get settled before then.

He followed them to their car, and smiled when they hummed together . . . in perfect harmony.

Thanks, God.

6

GRANGER TASTED THE sweet power and hungered for more.

Marty had spent the past few days trying to getting details out of Granger. He wanted the scoop before the doors opened at school. Granger had enjoyed being the one in control. He strung a frustrated Marty along, teasing him with info about their battle at Demon's Bluff.

Finally he had mercy and spilled the story, skipping the details about his cowardice and jumping straight to his heroic finish.

"I did it up big," he said. Marty looked skeptical. "I ripped rocks loose and whaled them at this monster demon named Trevor. His foot was crushing Nancy." He didn't feel much emotion about her pain, but was thrilled to tell the tale of his victory. "You know I'm a sports star; basketball's my specialty. But let's just say I excel at anything I try." He had to work that in.

"Yeah—let's say that, whether or not it's true." Marty had uncrossed his arms. He was listening—although Granger could tell he didn't believe the part about demons.

"So this thing was stomping poor little Nancy to smithereens while *I* peppered him with missiles. Just me and only me. The rest were huddled in the dirt." He showed Marty where everyone had been positioned. He was having fun. "I hadn't thrown so many projectiles since baseball season. I kept scooping and firing, scooping and firing."

"What'd the . . . *demon* do?"

"That's where it got interesting." Granger pulled himself to his full six-feet-one-inch height. "He came at me. Roaring with the most disgusting breath—even worse than yours."

Marty wasn't amused. "So it was you against the ultimate forces of evil?" He smirked.

"No doubt." Granger kept his voice upbeat. In his mind he saw the angels coming to his rescue, stepping in and saving the day. But Marty hadn't been there. He couldn't know the truth—not that he'd believe it. "So I stood my ground, knocked Trevor to the ground. Dead."

"Cool."

"Got that right."

Granger felt a little guilty about lying, but so what? Marty wanted a story, so he'd given him one.

He passed along another interesting tidbit.

"Claudia's a Christian?" Marty lost it and began laughing.

Granger spun the shiny ring on his finger. "Yup, she's one of them."

Marty wiped his eyes. "She's the one who used to tease you about seeing little dragons jumping around on my head. Remember?"

Granger nodded. "Well, if you're not interested . . . Just thought you told me you get extra credit for each Christ-Kid you turn over to the WPA."

"Yeah. Sure." Marty stood straight, all official. He was listening. "But I need proof."

"Don't we all?"

McCRY WAS GONE but something about her stayed in the room. A buzzing tingle that made it impossible for Erin to stay in her seat.

"How can you do this to Patch?" Erin said.

"You watch your tone," her father replied.

"I'm sorry. I don't mean to be disrespectful. But how could you keep this from him? And why?"

"You know how difficult it was to have one of those kids in this house, let alone two," her mother said.

"You seriously don't think Patch deserved to know?"

Her mom's face twisted. "We didn't owe Patrick Johnson anything. We gave him a home and food, all out of the goodness of our hearts."

Another fib. Erin knew her parents had allowed Patch into their home only because they got money from the government.

"Where will Jenny stay?"

"With you, of course." Mr. Morgan carried the dishes into the kitchen.

"You were close to him," her mom said. "You can bond with her."

The doorbell rang.

Her mother flashed another smile. "That'll be her now."

THAT ONE, RIGHT there." Ma Stone pointed to a three-story Victorian house with lacy curtains at the windows. "Should have been ours." Her voice sounded soft. She turned to Patch. "Don't you think it's elegant?"

Patch didn't have much opinion one way or the other. "Seems nice."

"I still don't see why God didn't give it to us." Ma Stone was pouting.

"Now, sweet stuff, you've got a home already." Patch saw the man pat her shoulder. "You can't go second-guessing God."

"You're right, honey." The last word sounded like a bird call.

"And I bet that big old mansion doesn't have its very own Seclusion Point in the back." He kept his eyes on the road, but Patch saw that the woman was smiling again.

"Course not." She put her hands in her lap. "I'm perfectly content." She looked at the slowly passing green lawns, dogs barking alongside the car. "Why wouldn't I be?"

Patch had no idea what to say, so he kept quiet. These two were strange. Nice, but definitely a little off.

After the slow-motion drive through town to show him around, the Stones finally brought Patch home. Inside, he looked around the front room. Not at all what he'd expected. With all the recordings done by Ma and Pa Stone, he'd thought to find himself in a mansion like the one Ma Stone had pointed out. This place barely looked livable. The front room was crammed with furniture. Oversized for obvious reasons, but leaving very little walking space.

Along the walls were shelves full of pictures. Windows were blocked to make room for knickknacks galore. There were photos of the Stones with fans, the Stones on stage, and a framed copy of their mega bestseller album *The Stones Underground.* Lots of awards too. Shiny silver statues, see-through acrylic scepters. Apparently, they'd never thrown a single thing away.

"Incredible." Patch said the first word that came to his mouth. "Lots of memories, I suppose."

"We've been blessed, that's for sure," Pa Stone said. He pulled a scrapbook off a shelf. "I think there's time before dinner." He smiled at his wife.

Patch examined the cover. "Bible Belt Tour 1990." Talk about a blast from the past.

Ma Stone gestured to the couch. Though the furniture was supersized, the piece seemed barely big enough for the three of them. Patch sat in the middle and they crowded in on both sides. Snug. That's how he felt.

They opened the first page of the scrapbook and Ma Stone began reminiscing. "You remember that couple and their children? How they brought us a dozen roses?"

"That was years before the WPA clamped down so hard on musical expression."

Ma and Pa Stone took turns pointing to numerous faces, slowly turning the pages while Patch squirmed. How many of these stories would he have to suffer through before supper? He could barely breathe. At least they didn't have scrapbooks full of pictures of kids. Ma Stone had said it wasn't "God's will" that they have children of their own, but that they sure hoped Patch would be able to stay a while.

When the book finally shut, Ma Stone stood and turned on a CD. Definitely not Patch's style, but nice anyway—tight harmonies, old-fashioned lyrics.

"That's us." She fluttered her fingers before her face.

"Don't be so modest," Pa Stone said. "We can still belt out a tune. After dinner we'll give the boy a concert."

Patch could hardly wait.

7

CLAUDIA HAD NOT been happy when she got Erin's call saying she couldn't make the meeting after all. This was going to be tough enough as it was. Molly had sounded strange on the phone. And she already knew Nancy was no friend.

When the others showed, she started the meeting in her cramped living room with her cat snoozing in her lap.

Nancy jumped right in. "So it was urgent for us, but not for Erin?"

"Last-minute company," Claudia said. "She wanted to be here."

"Obviously."

This was going exactly as Claudia feared it would.

"So what if Erin can't make it?" Molly said, black hair pulled into a ponytail. "There's nothing to talk about."

Nancy looked bored.

Claudia was desperate. "We have to talk. Get our stories straight."

Molly's face reddened. "That's all this is to you, isn't it?"

"I'm as much a Christian as you are," Claudia said.

"Obviously, we won't make any decision without Erin," Nancy said, looking at Molly. Claudia wanted to slap her. "And you, Claw, have probably already arranged to make yourself look good."

"What?"

"Don't deny it," Nancy said. "Have you seen Marty yet?"

"I didn't know he was back in town," Claudia said.

"You're lying," Nancy said, poking a finger at her. "Marty has been hanging around with Granger since he got back. And we all know what good friends you and Granger are."

"Once and for all, I'm not interested in Granger."

Molly said, "Let's get down to the issue. You and Erin think we should shut up about the whole Christian thing?"

"For now," Claudia said. "We have to know what it'll cost us if everyone finds out."

Molly stood, gesturing. "Forget it. I know what I know. I saw what I saw. And I won't turn my back on my faith."

She was gone.

"I don't get you," Nancy said. "It was a whole lot easier when you were a creep. School starts next Monday. I'm getting back on track—Demon's Bluff or not."

GRANGER WATCHED MARTY twitch. Nervous guy. The two of them sat in a dark car, passing a covert listening device back and forth. Not that it did them any good—the range on the thing was terrible.

"I thought you said there were four of 'em."

Granger slammed Marty on the back. "You saw Nancy and Molly leaving Claudia's house. Remember how well they got along?"

"Girls are flaky." Marty leaned back. "Them getting together means nothing. Certainly isn't going to earn me any credit with the WPA. Especially since we have no idea what they talked about."

Granger rolled the ring around on his finger, studied the etched winged beast. He knew exactly what they'd said. *But why wasn't Erin there?* "So you need more evidence?"

"What's with your ring?" Marty grabbed Granger's hand and yanked.

"Knock it off."

Marty held Granger's hand firmly and stared at the ring's markings. Granger couldn't free himself. Marty was strong. No way could he best him in a fight.

Good thing he could read Marty's mind. The guy was mad. He wanted something concrete to take to McCry. Confessions.

That might take some time, Marty, Granger thought. The guy needed to learn a little patience.

JENNY JOHNSON HELD out a thin wrist and smiled. Her eyes reminded Erin of Patch.

"Do you like my watch?" Her small white teeth gleamed.

Erin gave the girl a hug. "Very much."

"Everyone does." Jenny breathed onto the pastel timepiece and rubbed it clean.

Erin wondered if that were true. "What time is it?"

Jenny appeared to study the numbers. "I don't know."

"It's a pretty watch," Erin said. She noticed the second hand was frozen at ten o'clock. She decided against asking about it.

Jenny nodded, smiling her big brother's broad grin. "Pink's my favorite color." She touched Erin's arm. "Mommy and Daddy gave me this watch. It's all I have left from them."

THE PEACEFUL ONE watched Jenny crawl into Erin's lap. Some comfort for the child, but would it last? That the angel could not answer.

He had been there when the child's parents fell. Had seen the little one, even smaller then, curl deeper into her father's arms. Watched her tears.

But she wasn't left alone. The angel had nudged the WPA woman that long-ago night at Parkway Mall. The woman snatched the child from her father and took her to safety. The Peaceful One had made sure of that.

Since then, the girl had been shuttled from home to home, never finding a place. Perhaps this would be a new start.

The Peaceful One hoped so.

8

SCHOOL BELLS WOULD clang tomorrow, but Claudia wasn't too worried. By now she'd gotten the whole back-to-class thing down pat. It was Sunday night and Claudia was going to relax. Right now she and Erin were walking through the park while Claudia updated Erin on the meeting she missed, the gathering of the female Demon's Bluff survivors. She didn't hold any details back.

"A nightmare," Claudia said. "At least this time I could see who was attacking."

Erin laughed. "Sorry I couldn't be there."

Claudia expected Erin to say more, but she didn't. "No, you aren't," Claudia said. "Maybe it was for the best." The two stopped to watch the ducks. "But now we've got a clear picture of where the others stand."

"You have to admire Molly," Erin said.

"She's honest—but crazy."

"Maybe we should follow her lead."

Something was bugging Erin. Claudia hoped she'd open up. She stooped and fingered the cool water. "Think what would happen to us at school if everyone knew."

"The same thing that happened to Patch?"

"I miss having him around. Things were more exciting."

"Might get that way again. His little sister is alive and living in my home."

"What?" Claudia demanded all the information Erin had.

"McCry's got her eye on me."

"That's never good," Claudia said.

NONE OF YOUR business." Nancy was sick of being pushed around. Even by Granger and especially on the first day of school. Talk about humiliating. Kids scrambled through the hallways, pushing and shouting.

"That's no way for my girlfriend to act." Granger opened a bag of chips.

"Thanks for letting me know."

"That you were being rude?" Granger glanced at his ring.

"No. That I was your girlfriend."

"Bet I know what you're thinking," he said.

At least he'd called her "girlfriend." That was worth something. Nancy slipped her arm through Granger's. "I'm sure you do."

9

E RIN CHECKED HER mirror, ready to hurry to her first class. Good thing school was close or she'd be late. But before she could leave she heard Jenny wailing, "Keep her away from me." Seconds later the little girl ran in and burrowed into Erin's side. Erin looked up and saw McCry in her bedroom doorway.

"Your mother let me in," McCry said. "Gave me an extra key. So I can keep tabs on this little one, make sure she's okay in her new home. You understand I need to keep tabs on that." She stroked Jenny's hair. The girl slapped her hand.

"Don't let her take me!"

"You're safe here," Erin said, deliberately shielding Jenny from McCry.

"As long as you follow the rules," McCry said as she started for the door, "you'll both be fine."

Something in Erin snapped. No matter the consequences, she was going to let McCry have it. She followed the woman out the door and to her car. "I don't know what you're up to, but I'm going to make sure you don't win. I don't want you coming back here, messing with my family. Or Patch's sister."

McCry smirked as she got into her car. "Don't get so upset." She checked her makeup in the rearview mirror. "Get Patch back here. Once he's in my custody you can do whatever you want with the girl."

"Her name's Jenny."

"I know. We're going to use her to find her brother."

"I won't let you," Erin said.

Without warning, McCry grabbed her around the throat, cutting off her air. Erin couldn't even cough. "You won't behave like this again. Ever."

The next second Erin was free and McCry was looking up and down the tree-lined street to see if anyone had noticed their little scene. Erin hacked away until air flowed back down her windpipe.

"I know what you are—and what you pretend to be," McCry said.

Erin was having trouble thinking, probably because of the attack. Did McCry mean she was acting brave when she really wasn't? Or Christian when she didn't have a clue? Both were definitely true.

McCry's cold eyes bored into her, and Erin knew she'd reached her limit. She shivered. But it didn't matter. Erin's mission was clear at this point: somehow, some way, she would find a way to reunite Patch and Jenny.

THIS WAS AN incredible school. Small classes, friendly teachers, kids who shared homemade cookies at lunch. What more could he want?

Patch had already met a couple of great guys. They were Christians too. Open about their faith. "Guess it was God's will that we meet," said the one wearing glasses.

"Must be," the other kid said. Tall and wearing a white T-shirt.

Made sense. And besides, Patch was just glad to have someone to hang around with. He was tired of being lonely.

"And can you believe he's living with Ma and Pa Stone?" said T-Shirt.

"Talk about lucky," Glasses said.

"I've heard they're pretty famous." Patch didn't want to sound proud, but these two must have thought the Stones were a big deal.

"They're legends." Glasses picked at something in his teeth. "I love their music almost as much as my grandparents do."

Great for them. Maybe the Stones would put on a little concert for his friends sometime, like they did for him. They were obviously willing to perform at the drop of a hint.

He'd just have to see how things worked out.

ONE DAY OF school finished, too many left to count. Marty and Granger stretched out on Granger's bedroom carpet, gulping down candy bars. Marty didn't say a word. All the same, Granger knew.

"You need more proof."

"Stop that," Marty said. "At least let me say what I'm thinking before you respond."

Maybe Granger had made a mistake in telling Marty about the ring. But it was the only thing Granger could think of to prove himself.

"Sorry. Keep forgetting it's impolite to scan your brain."

"So you've been listening. Illegally, inappropriately."

Granger smiled. He hadn't realized Marty even knew such a long word as *inappropriately*. "I saw a WPA truck outside Erin's house today."

Marty scratched his head. "So she's going to try to find a way to contact Patch?"

"No. She's going to double-cross McCry. Help that little girl."

Marty checked his at-attention hair in the mirror. "McCry's a good friend of mine." He shrugged.

"I'll stay close to Nancy." Granger fiddled with the ring. "I don't need to read her mind. She tells me everything."

THE FIRST WEEK of school was creeping by. Things hadn't changed much since she was in elementary school. Claudia still lived for lunch. Now that she packed it herself and avoided Mom's gross lunchmeat surprises, she liked the break even better.

Lonely Girl straight ahead.

Claudia crossed to where Molly sat staring at the empty seats around her. The most beautiful girl in high school, sitting alone at lunch. Claudia knew why. Molly's fan club had shriveled since she started talking about Jesus.

"I didn't think you'd care to be seen with me," Molly said.

Claudia kept her voice low. "We're on the same team. I just think a different approach is better."

Molly bit her apple. "Hero or coward. Those are the only options."

"Everyone faces a different situation."

"No. There are lies and there's the Truth. You're still spouting the same relativistic garbage they've been shoveling us since we were in kindergarten."

"Even Christians don't agree on everything."

"On certain issues there's no room for compromise." Molly stood and excused herself.

All Claudia could do was stand there and wonder who was right.

10

"Mom," Erin said, "I'm telling the truth." Would this happen every night? Her parents stood over her bed as she pulled her covers up. "I do *not* know where Patch is." Why were they interrogating her?

"Ms. McCry is certain you could get in touch with him."

Her father said, "Don't you want him to see his sister again?"

Erin sat up and crossed her arms. "Can't we give her a little time before we rock her world again?"

"You don't get it. If we help catch him, the reward will be remarkable." Mrs. Morgan had no emotion in her voice. "We'll share with you, of course."

That's why they were doing this. "She's a scared little girl." Erin wanted to shake her parents, get them to see for once.

"She's a criminal. Why should we care what happens to her?"

Such coldness. Erin gazed at her mom, half expecting to see frost form on her lips.

Another tack. "Terry loves her too. It's so great to see them playing together."

"Someday you'll understand. Till then you'll just have to trust us."

Disgusted, her parents left her room. With a sigh, Erin got up and turned on her computer, searching the Internet for any sign of Patch. Nothing. That was the irony: McCry wanted her to contact Patch, and here Erin had been hoping McCry would be the one to lead her to him. Neither of them knew where Patch was.

And it wasn't likely he was going to contact Erin himself.

Erin would just have to figure it out on her own.

ONLY THE THIRD day of school and Granger was already having fun. Just that morning he'd aced a pop vocabulary quiz. He read the answers one at a time from the smart girl in his class. Molly, the Do-Gooder. Wonder what she'd say if she knew that he knew she was a Christian. Would she want everyone else to know?

He pretended to be scratching his thoughts out on paper. But he was stealing, watching her mind form sprawling cursive and then copying her responses on his own test.

After class he rushed the snack machine. Nancy lurked, waiting for him. He didn't have to know what she was thinking. Her intentions were obvious.

"You don't really think you can pull it off, do you?" Granger sat at a table and ate a cookie while Nancy tugged at his ring.

"Why don't you take it off?" Nancy glared at the band on his finger.

He thought she should smile more. "I like it," he said.

"I got rid of mine. It would be nice to talk without worrying that you're reading my mind."

"I know," he said, smiling.

What she didn't know was that he'd already learned everything he needed. It was time to report to Marty.

He blew Nancy a kiss, then smiled at her reaction. "Yeah, I know," he said. "I think you're pretty amazing too."

"You got that one wrong," Nancy said.

"Close enough."

She shook her head, but Granger knew better. She found him irresistible.

Evening. Mom-and-daughter connection time. Claudia cleared her throat. "Mom, can we talk?" Claudia did not want to have this conversation, but what choice did she have?

Her mom looked like she'd had a rough day at work. Claudia passed her a tall glass of iced cola and got a surprised look in return.

"I know you said I should wait, Mom, but I don't think I can keep silent any longer."

"So you're willing to destroy me, ruin my career, all because of some desert religious experience?"

"What if Christianity is the answer?"

Her mother snorted. "It's the wrong answer for me. I know that much."

"But what if you're wrong?"

Claudia's mom nibbled her fingernail. "You think you've got it figured out. Life. The big picture." She jammed her hand in her jeans pocket. "I'm almost fifty and I still don't know what's going on."

What an opening. Claudia didn't want to blow it. "Mom, I felt the same way when I went to Demon's Bluff. Like I didn't have a clue."

"That's not what I said. You're always trying to put words in my mouth." She walked to the couch. "I know a whole lot more than you do, young lady."

Claudia hadn't meant to upset her. Why did she always seem to say the wrong thing? She only wanted to be clear.

"That's not what I'm saying." Claudia took a quiet breath, said a prayer. "So tell me, Mom. Please." She wasn't playing a game. She really wanted to know. "What's the secret to true happiness? Because I haven't seen it in this house."

"You're not being fair." Her mom lay down.

"Maybe, but I'm trying to be honest." Sensing the moment had passed, Claudia leaned down and kissed her mom on the forehead. Hopefully they'd have more time to talk later.

11

WEDNESDAY AFTERNOON, AND school was out. Patch sat on a small bench in the Stones' backyard, staring absently at the words: "Seclusion Point." That's what the small wooden sign said. Someone had burned each letter into the rickety piece of board and hung it between two posts. A concrete bench sat beneath.

"Pa Stone made that for me. Said he'd do a lot of woodworking when he retired." Ma Stone walked over to Patch. "Got busy with other things."

"I like it." Patch tapped the sign with a finger and it jangled.

"This is my favorite spot in the world." Patch made room for her and she sat beside him. "And I've seen enough to know. Every year I watch my sunflowers grow."

Other climbing plants grew along the fence—blue and pink blooms. It was an oasis of color in an otherwise plain yard.

"So do you and Pa Stone like to travel?"

She gave him a funny look. "Would if we could." She gestured to the rest of the small yard. Patch noticed the bare spots, the weeds sneaking past the slats in the wood fence. "I think we deserve a bit more than this."

"Peaceful here." Patch wanted to change the subject.

Turning, she smiled. "It reminds me of the gardens in Seclusion Point, Kauai. That's what this place is named for." She swayed her arms like a hula dancer and Patch laughed.

"Pa and I loved singing on the islands." She patted Patch's knee. "We were so popular back then." She sighed. "If only we'd saved a bit more when we had it. Anyway, when Pa saw how much I loved the place in Hawaii, he planted this corner with every flower he could find."

Patch sat back listening, unwilling to interrupt.

"I like to sit here and pray. Used to do a lot more weeding myself." She smoothed her muumuu over her knees. "Now I mostly take my worries to the Lord. Let Pa do the garden work."

Patch looked around again. The flowers smelled sweet. "Do you mind if I come here sometimes?"

Ma Stone began humming. Patch didn't know the song. "'I Come to the Garden Alone,'" she said in answer to his curious look. "I think Man misses Eden, so we're always looking for a piece of that memory. Our own little quiet spot."

Patch didn't know about that, but he was glad to learn a bit more about this woman. "Thanks for the story."

"You're welcome at Seclusion Point any time." She tipped her head and smiled. "I'm going to stay a while longer." She looked toward the sunflowers, then bowed her head.

NEW SCHOOL YEAR, new agenda. McCry had had enough with the rebellion. Christianity was illegal, and yet pockets of believers still infested the country. As was typical, bigger cities followed the rules immediately. Smaller towns proved more independent. That made it tougher to catch renegades and punish them.

Renegades like Patch.

The problem was McCry did not have enough staff focused on her priorities.

Where was Marty? Ah, there he was, the bumbling fool. He ran in the door, handed her a cup of coffee. She sipped. Three sugars kept her sweet. The teen was learning. He left the room again, heading back to the kitchen.

"We need a way to bring them to us," McCry called after him. "What do you think about an essay contest? Cash always attracts kids."

"We all need money."

Marty was right.

McCry explained that they could leak a story to the media about the WPA loosening anti-religion laws. She could even mention Patch by name, talk about how she hated to see such a young man so obviously confused.

"Brilliant. How can I help?" Marty returned with a plate and fawned all over her, acting like it was the best idea he'd ever heard. McCry took the plate from him. She loved having this macho officer-in-training warm up toaster strudel for her.

Marty also wanted to know the topic of the essay.

The topic? What would work? McCry bit her lip, thinking. "Why the world needs God." If people were foolish enough to believe the WPA was considering a policy change, the entries could be numerous.

"I don't suppose the winner will actually collect the prize," Marty said, scratching his fuzzy head.

"I don't have a problem with that," McCry said. "Do you?"

He waited until she laughed, then joined in.

12

NEARLY A MONTH had flown by. Patch had settled into his school routine, homework every afternoon. Today Ma Stone popped in with a question. "You like to write?" Pa Stone stood listening at the doorway.

"I try not to miss a day in my journal." Patch shut his book.

"That's what Henry and I thought. Have you heard about the WPA contest?"

She explained the prize would be enough to remodel the entire house. Her deep-set eyes sparkled. "Maybe in gratitude for having a place to stay, you might be willing to enter for us?"

She looked so hopeful, Patch had a hard time saying no. But the thought of any connection with McCry made his skin crawl. "It has to be a trap."

"So's this place." She waved her hand. "A rat trap. After all our service to the Lord, you'd think we'd have a nicer place." Her head dropped.

"It's the Lord's will, sweetums." Pa Stone crossed to her, patted her shoulder.

"I think his will is for the boy to put us first. Win that money." Her eyes narrowed.

Patch wouldn't have been surprised if she'd started rubbing her hands together.

"It's perfectly legitimate." She waggled the *Sticklerville Gazette*. "There's an entry form in the paper."

She showed him the article. When he barely glanced at the contents, she left in a huff, Pa Stone behind her.

The Tattooed Rats vouched for these folks, but after that strange scene, Patch felt worried. Maybe he should risk contacting Gary, give him an update.

Erin was ready for a break. They'd survived the first month of school without any demons dropping from the sky. Nothing too exciting happened in class. Saturday night almost seemed like a letdown.

Because of their differing schedules it was the first time Nancy, Erin, Claudia, and Molly had all gotten together since their return from Demon's Bluff. The WPA essay contest was all they talked about. Erin was thrilled. "Don't you realize what this means? Christianity could be on the brink of a comeback!"

"I thought Jesus always stayed the same," Molly said, pacing.

"My parents don't want me to have anything to do with it," Nancy said. "That's lucky for you, Erin. Otherwise I'm sure I would win." She stuck her nose up. "I could buy a lot of books with the money."

"Why so quiet, Claudia?" Erin said.

"My mom. I think she's close to becoming a believer."

"That's great," Molly said.

"Would you pray for her?" Claudia asked. "And for me?"

"Maybe you could write about the struggle to believe," Erin said. "About how every person should have the right to make the decision for herself."

"One thing, though," Molly said, grinning. "Those who enter will make easy targets for the WPA." She looked like she enjoyed that thought.

Erin thought Molly was crazy.

"I'll be happy to edit your writing," Nancy said, "but don't expect me to put myself and my family on the line." She left, claiming she had to go to the library.

The remaining three looked at each other. "Granger," they said as one.

I'VE BEEN WRITING for hours." Patch said. "What about you? Have you started yet?"

T-Shirt scratched his nose. Patch knew the guy's name was Leon, but he still thought of him as T-Shirt. That's all he wore. He had one in every color of the rainbow, plus an unlimited number of plain white ones. "Yeah. I worked till midnight." He snickered.

Glasses, also known as Denny, muttered in Patch's direction, "Show off."

"What are you talking about?" Patch was offended. He didn't want to write the essay either, but what choice did he have?

"I thought you said you believed in God," Leon said.

The comment zipped past Patch like a fly ball. "I have to write an essay so I sit down and type." What did that have to do with God?

"If it's really God's will, you shouldn't have to work at it," Denny said. "Least not very hard."

Is this how these guys handled homework? Waiting for the answers to drop from the skies? It made no sense to Patch.

Leon gestured to himself. "Look. You can try to force things to happen. Or you can let God have his way."

Denny gave Patch a sideways glance. "We show trust. Never force things."

"So what you're saying is that neither of you have started writing." Patch just wanted to be clear on this point. They both looked down.

"When God's ready to give us the words, we'll be happy to jot them down." Leon pointed toward a pick-up basketball game. "C'mon. Stop worrying."

Patch liked basketball, but he knew he'd better keep scribbling away on his essay. "Maybe later."

He watched them turn their backs on him. Were they really showing faith—or just being lazy?

WHAT DID I tell you?" Granger asked. He stopped the recording device Nancy had worn and handed the disk to Marty. "Good job, Nancy," he said.

"Did you like how I offered to help them improve their essays?" she said.

Granger rolled his eyes. "Clever."

He hardly needed to use the ring with her. She had such a crush on him. Not his fault. He had moved on. Now, when he thought it over, he didn't get what he'd seen in her. So slouchy, grumpy, whiney.

"You don't think this contest is for real, do you?" Marty said. "It's just a way for them to find some imbeciles. They won't go after everybody. Just a select few."

"But this tape is genuine," Granger said. "Should get you in good with McCry."

"Like I need it."

Granger shook his head ever so slightly. But enough for Marty to shut up and think. Realize that Mighty Granger knew all. "Okay, fine. I need it bad. Wanna get promoted—and fast."

SHAPE-SHIFTING FOR Experts.'"

Sure, Hope had already graduated. But she hadn't been about to pass up this special session—not if what she learned helped her practice evil more efficiently.

She shrank down to the size of a dragonfly. A pretty, shiny one.

This was how she and Barry would travel when they had to escape unseen. Or if they hadn't swallowed up enough fear. She hated getting small, but when the humans didn't project terror in large enough volumes, they made do.

Of course when they were in human form, they used the standard means of transportation. Plane, train, automobile. But that could be so slow.

Hope worked on improving her technique, snickering under her breath as she watched Barry. He had agreed to take the class after she bugged him, but he wasn't doing so well with it. At the moment, his tiny head was shriveled to the size of a pea, but his body remained huge and out of proportion.

She shook her wings to hide her laughter.

Then came a loud *pop* and his distorted body crinkled down. He matched, looking like a bee on steroids.

"Buzz off," Hope said. She practiced making lazy loops in the starry sky.

13

Erin watched her brother and Jenny play as though they had grown up together. Terry was kindhearted and sometimes let Jenny have her own way too quickly. But becoming the little princess didn't spoil her; it just made her more benevolent herself.

Erin had to laugh when she saw them play tea party. This was how kids were supposed to spend their days—having fun, not worrying about the end of the world.

"What do you remember about Patch, Jenny?" Erin said.

"She knows Patch?" Terry asked.

Erin realized he'd never made the connection. "Jenny is Patch's sister," Erin said.

"Really?" Terry said. "I love Patchy."

Jenny nodded, grinning. "Patch was my brother."

Hearing the past tense, Erin realized the girl might not know Patch was alive. Maybe that was for the best. What if they never got together again?

Jenny crawled into her lap, begging for a story. Erin opened a book, wishing she had a collection of children's Bible stories with lots of pictures. Jenny would love that.

Holding the little girl in her arms strengthened Erin's resolve. She had a plan. She'd considered all the options. No matter what the woman said, McCry, with all of her tracking tools, would never have lost track of Patch. The WPA had all the power. That meant Marty might have access to the information too. Now that he was one of them.

She'd get Nancy to ask Granger to ask Marty where Patch was. What could be simpler?

Yeah, right.

But even if Marty was unwilling to talk, Granger could read his mind. Her plan wouldn't work, though, unless she knew for sure that Nancy was on her side.

PATCH SNUCK HIS cell phone from his backpack in the closet. He hadn't had any occasion to use it yet. Now he was glad it was around. He dialed.

"Gary . . . I'm a little . . . concerned." Patch didn't want to sound like he was whining. He took a breath and explained how at first everything had seemed fine. He spoke about Leon and Denny's strange attitude. And then he turned to his bigger concern—the Stones. "They've turned way weird. Seem obsessed with me entering that WPA essay contest about God. Always complaining about not having enough money."

"Our intelligence still doesn't know if that contest is legit or not." Gary's voice sounded calm. "But still, maybe you're supposed to enter it."

Patch wished they could talk face to face. "But you know it's got to be a scam. McCry's attempt to find Christians in hiding."

"Could be. Or maybe it's part of God's plan."

Patch didn't get Gary's attitude. "Why bother, then?" Now he sounded like his friends T-Shirt and Glasses. Maybe they were right to let things slide.

"Because it might be what God wants you to do." Gary cleared his throat. "Even if you don't want to."

"And I don't."

"Then I guess you probably should. Lots of times God tells me to do the exact thing I'm sure I can't do—or don't want to do." Gary laughed. "Seems like the way he teaches me the hard stuff."

"But you don't know what it's like with them." Patch realized he was acting like a baby.

"I'm sure you love those sing-alongs." Gary laughed. "Patch, listen to them. I'm sure they have your best interests at heart. Like I said, I've only heard great things about them. They're Christian singing superstars."

"Yeah." It was all Patch could say.

"I'm jealous."

"Say the word and I'll switch places."

Somehow, though, talking to Gary made him feel better. Maybe he was right. Maybe it was just that the Stones were on a pretty strict budget and had a taste for a few nicer things. What was wrong with that? Maybe he should help them out.

He sighed. "I'll stay."

"Glad you're trying to make it work," Gary said.

Marty was tired of the foolishness. These people he had known as classmates before summer break were now clearly inferior. WPA training had strengthened his mind and body, made him more discerning. Spending his afternoons with McCry had gotten him on the right track. If only he could find a way to move up the ranks quicker.

Though he was the same fun-loving Marty, he had more purpose now. Capturing renegade Christians topped his list. He wasn't going to come out of school with anything less than an officer position.

That's what McCry promised him—*if* he was able to gather evidence against the girls.

And if he couldn't trust McCry, who could he trust?

The task would be much easier if he had a ring like Granger's. Or if he could at least get the guy to give him a lead on another one. Marty wondered what McCry would offer if he delivered a ring of her own.

Granger shouldn't have bragged about the ring, letting others realize how valuable it was.

Oh, well. His mistake. If it got stolen, that would be his own fault.

14

AFTER MAKING HIS secret call to the Rats, Patch paced the sidewalk. He felt guilty talking about the Stones behind their backs. But this place was strange. People talked about following God's will like they knew without a doubt what it was. Patch wasn't even sure he'd recognize it.

But if this was what God had in store for him . . . guess he had no choice. Perhaps God was making things easier for him this time. And he was gumming things up. He should listen for a change.

Still, he wished he had more guidance from those he trusted. It was tough being without a home, without parents.

Across the street a boy pulled his sister in a red wagon, his legs moving like the wheels on a locomotive. Although he smiled to watch them, Patch was nervous. Why were those little kids allowed to play so close to a main street?

The little girl shrieked with delight. She reminded Patch of his own sister. He usually didn't let himself think about Jenny much. Sometimes he wondered if God kept him busy to keep his mind off the pain of losing her.

The boy took the corner sharply and zoomed around a shady elm. Cars zipped past. Patch's agitation grew.

Another quick corner. The wagon rose on two wheels. The girl laughed as if on a roller coaster. Something churned in Patch's stomach.

Faster and faster. The girl didn't sound so happy now. Was she crying? The boy looked exasperated. He turned too sharply and sent his sister flying.

Into the road.

In front of a car.

The driver had no chance to brake. And Patch recognized him.

Poor Pa Stone.

Patch covered his face when he heard the thud, the metal crunching. When he looked up again the little girl wasn't moving. Horrified, Patch screamed for help. He saw a man and woman sitting on a nearby bench. As Patch gestured in panic, the man got up and walked toward them.

Not waiting, Patch ran to the door of the police station. "Accident! A girl was hit by a car!" Barely checking for traffic, he tore across the street to the fire station. Four men in uniform stood staring. "Hurry!" Patch called.

Nobody moved. Why weren't they helping? It was surreal. He felt like everything was going in slow motion.

He ran back to the girl and lifted her head. She was breathing. Maybe she would be okay.

The Stones had gotten out of the car and now stood on the sidewalk looking at him strangely.

What was wrong with everybody?

"Put her down," the man from the bench said as he arrived.

Patch carefully lowered her head to the pavement. Her eyes fluttered.

"You have to leave her alone," the man said. His wife had followed and now stood there, her face blank.

"But . . . why?" Patch didn't understand their response. This was their own child. It seemed impossible that they would be standing there doing nothing.

Shaking his head in disbelief, Patch looked around and realized he was the only one trying to do anything. No one else moved. No one helped. They only stared, eyes dead.

The child's mom clutched her husband's arm. "It's God's will," she said. She repeated the phrase over and over. Not a prayer, but a chant. "It's God's will . . . It's God's will . . ." Her eyes stayed dry.

Patch looked at Ma and Pa Stone, but they shook their heads. He didn't get this. It was God's will that the girl die? That no one help?

As he sat there, the firemen turned back to the station. The policemen shook their heads and went back inside.

The father shoved Patch out of the way and scooped his daughter into his arms. As his wife followed, continuing her mantra, he walked down the street. The brother followed, pulling the wagon, tears streaming.

"You should not have butted in," Pa Stone said suddenly, his face grim. "Accidents happen. They're all part of God's plan." Ma Stone nodded, looking serene in her gold muumuu.

Patch was sickened. "But . . . But . . . will she be all right?" How could the Stones be so cold about everything? Pa Stone himself had hit the girl, yet he showed no remorse. What was wrong with him—with them?

"God knows about that little girl." Pa Stone yanked open the car door. "Get in. Time to go home. You've got an essay to write."

"That prize money is going to come in so handy," Ma Stone said.

Patch hesitated. It was all too much. It was as though these two people he'd lived with for a month were suddenly strangers to him. Strangers he didn't like.

Was this really what God had in mind for him—or the injured child?

Erin contacted Molly and Claudia and laid out her plan for finding Patch's whereabouts.

"The whole thing sounds crazy to me." Molly said, ponytail shaking.

Erin smiled. Good old Molly—you could always count on her to voice her opinion . . . strongly.

"It does seem a little complicated," Claudia said. "Like playing that 'Telephone' game and hoping to get a complete message at the end of the line. Nancy to Granger to Marty to McCry . . . Besides, can we even trust them to help?"

Their faces told her what they thought of her idea. "Okay, okay, I give up." Erin threw up her hands. "Give me a better idea. We've got to help Jenny find Patch. But where is he?"

"Don't you still have Jarrod's number?" Molly asked.

"Duh." She popped herself on the head. "It's in my call log." She pushed buttons on her phone, found the Demon's Bluff number, and tapped Send.

"Hello, Jarrod here."

Erin was excited. After introductions she said, "We're trying to get ahold of Patch."

Jarrod sounded instantly uncomfortable. "Not sure where he is. Sorry."

"It's important."

"So is keeping him safe."

Jarrod knew more than he was saying, but Erin understood why he might want to keep quiet. "Look. If you hear from him, please tell him to get in touch." Erin gave her cell number and e-mail address. "There's something I have to tell him."

After cordial good-byes, Jarrod hung up.

Still playing "Telephone," but getting a little closer.

The girls continued to debate their choices. Watching them, Erin realized how much they'd changed. Especially Claudia. Claudia carefully weighed her words. These days she was always concerned about the feelings of others, about saying the right thing. Nobody who'd known the Claw could doubt the difference in her.

"I don't think McCry's lying," Molly said. "Isn't that why she planted Jenny at your home? If she knew where Patch was, she wouldn't have to draw him to your house."

"Even if McCry doesn't know where Patch is now, she'd be the first to find out, wouldn't she?"

Molly shrugged. "Maybe. But the best thing we can do for Patch is win this essay contest. If we start speaking out about our faith, maybe it will be possible for Patch to return someday."

Go, Molly. She always wanted to make things better.

"Since we don't have to put our actual names on our entries," Claudia said, "maybe it *is* a good idea. We might be able to change some minds. Like my mom's."

Erin was glad the rules had changed, obviously to attract more entries. Claudia sounded more on board than before.

"I'm still using my real name," Molly said. "I'm not afraid to stand up for Christ."

Erin admired Molly, but she also knew there were different ways to express opinions. She and Claudia had decided to use code names, as the revised rules allowed.

"Someday," Molly said, "when you kneel before God, you are going to have to explain why you were afraid to let the world know where you stood."

To that Erin had no reply. That was between her and God.

"What about McCry?" Claudia said. "Do you think she cares about our commitment to God? She hates us because of what we believe."

"We don't have to be afraid of anyone if God's on our side."

"You think we're invincible?" Erin jumped in.

"No, just that we don't have to fear." Molly tipped her chin down. "We have God's protection for our souls. The rest of this"—she patted herself—"really doesn't matter all that much."

Erin knew she was right, but somehow the idea of never seeing

Patch again hurt. Deeply. She missed him. Not that he'd ever know that. The real reason she had to see him again was to tell him about Jenny.

Yeah, that was all.

15

WHAT AN EXHAUSTING day. First the accident, and then the Stones' strange reaction. Now they were acting as though nothing had happened. The table was full. White rolls and mounds of butter. A meaty casserole filled with cheesy rice sat at the center. Patch had already eyed trays of cookies and fudge in the kitchen.

Between mouthfuls, he said, "I still don't understand."

"We're Christians just like you. You can hear our sincerity in our songs. Isn't that right, Henry?" Ma Stone looked at her husband. "Who are you to judge our ways?" Her smile scared Patch.

"I don't mean to. I just don't understand why no one helped her."

Ma Stone made an O with her mouth. She looked to her husband.

"Heard of the Golden Rule?" Pa Stone said, wiping his mouth.

Patch nodded.

"Those folks were doing what they would've wanted done for them. We believe everything happens for a purpose. Same way God makes some of us rich—and some of us mighty poor." He cleared his throat. "God uses accidents too. They're part of his plan."

"Let's not talk about it anymore. All right?" Ma Stone stuffed a buttery roll into her mouth. Patch knew better than to argue.

Hope looked down at the sprawling suburbs. "As good a place to start as any, Barry," she said. "It's what Trevor would've done."

"Who needs Trevor?" Barry said.

It was true. Hope wondered why she'd ever feared Trevor. She and Barry had begun to bond when they realized their teacher, Trevor, wanted to shred them. But in the end he'd been all bulk and no bite. Teeth and claws without much brain. Now he was gone. Zapped flat by a lucky angel strike. And they were free to make their own plans.

Tiny as ticks they landed behind the high school and slipped into their costumes. The transformation process quickened each time. They'd been practicing. This time they were wearing teen skins with more up-to-date clothes. A way better look for them.

"So how do I look?" Barry popped up from behind a dumpster. He'd gone for a classic polo shirt. Pale blue. Prep-school cool.

"Not bad. How about me?" Hope curtsied, flaring out her skirt.

Barry whistled. "Nice hair."

"And never needs washing."

"Your beauty is truly skin deep." Hope hissed. "Just kidding. Your true beauty lies way beneath the surface." She'd shown him. He knew.

Hope preened, then smirked. They not only looked like the real deal, they sounded like it. The pair had taken pains to improve their patter. They'd never pass for real teens if they sounded too immature.

"First stop, Granger," she said.

Because the school was so large, it could take weeks before anyone realized they never went to class. They staked out the cafeteria.

"Think he'll recognize us?" Barry asked.

"No way. His mind is an unpurified mess. Besides, we've got a whole new look, new attitude. Just watch." She strutted to the vending machines. Barry followed.

Just then Granger entered the cafeteria, followed by a sullen Nancy.

"Why have you been avoiding me, Granger?" she whined.

As Granger shrugged, Hope smiled. This was going to be easy.

"Annoying Nancy," Barry whispered. "Wasn't that what Trevor called her?"

"That's what everyone called her," Hope replied.

Nancy fussed some more, but Granger ignored her. He'd seen Hope. *Good boy*, she thought.

Hope had Granger's complete attention as she slipped coins into a vending machine. Nancy, pale and plain, looked upset as usual. Hope checked Granger's hands. No sign of the ring. Interesting. That must mean he'd figured out how to take the ring on and off. He was learning.

THE NEXT DAY Patch saw the boy kicking stones outside the hospital. It was the kid who had accidentally tossed his sister in front of a car. Patch had hardly slept for worrying about the child.

"How's she doing?" Patch said.

The boy looked up. "Who?"

"Your sister."

The child's eyes watered. "Stay away from me."

His father approached. "You." He hurried toward Patch. "Get out of here right now. Leave my son alone."

"I just wondered how your daughter is doing."

"God is with her. That boy is learning a good lesson."

"And what's that?"

Patch got a glare in return. "God's ways are not our ways."

"I've been praying for her," Patch said.

The man scratched his ear and turned away. "Thanks," he said, without looking back.

BARRY WASN'T WORRIED. Although he was not too experienced in the ways of the human world, it was obvious to him Hope had things under control. The school, and Granger, would be eating out of her hand. He caught a city bus to McCry's office. The WPA headquarters flew a huge flag marked with a red peace symbol from the top of the domed building.

The woman at the desk seemed impressed with Barry's phony credentials and buzzed McCry. While he waited, the woman offered him chilled water. He turned her down. Demons preferred hot liquids.

Ms. McCry looked the same. Of course she'd forgotten him. It was just as Flabbygums had said—memories leaking from the weak-minded.

Of course, the new disguise helped.

After scanning his paperwork she offered him an internship, believing he was recommended by the big bosses at federal head-quarters.

"Don't you need to get back to school?" McCry said.

"The principal thinks this is more important. He gave me after-noons off." Barry leaned close and sensed her discomfort. He knew that something about him troubled her. "Hope that's okay with you." He felt her fear growing. She was mean. That's why Trevor liked her, why Barry knew he'd get along with her. But she was weak as well.

"Certainly." She sat back in her chair. "We want to encourage bright young men."

If she only knew. Demons didn't age. What lurked beneath his teen-idol image was the real Barry, a crusty old monster.

He hoped to introduce his inner self to McCry soon.

A tall guy, clean-cut, approached. McCry introduced him as Marty. Barry sensed the guy was jealous. But why?

"Barry will be gathering information on Patrick Johnson," McCry said, giving Marty an annoyed look. To Barry she added, "So far, our intelligence efforts have been less than successful."

"Is he experienced?" Marty walked around Barry.

Time to make a scene. "Well, I know *you* are working for a superstar."

Barry poked a finger into Marty's taut chest. "I bet she's too modest to tell you everything." McCry sat up straighter. "She captured a spy called Trevor."

He'd heard the story from Trevor back at Demon's Bluff. Barry went into detail about how McCry had stopped her car for Trevor as he was trying to escape Demon's Bluff and made him return to town. He exaggerated the incident—and left out the part where Trevor had turned on her and scared her when he exposed his demon self.

McCry lapped it up. Apparently it was impossible to embarrass the woman.

Marty's eyes had widened. "Is all that true?"

McCry's silence spoke volumes.

Barry watched as Marty's mouth twisted. He had created a new enemy. The teacher's pet hated being shown up. And Barry had proven he had access to insider information.

THE MOMENT PATCH stepped out of the muggy heat into the cool air-conditioning, he knew something was wrong.

"I won't have that in this house." Ma Stone was weeping, scrunching up a handkerchief and loudly blowing her nose.

What have I done this time? Patch wondered.

"We agreed it was God's will to bring him here." Pa Stone kept his voice low. "And you know we weren't the only ones trying to get the boy placed in our home."

"But what will the neighbors say?" his wife said.

"The kind ones will understand." He took her hand. "Who cares what the nasty ones think?"

The Stones turned toward Patch, a wall of sad-eyed irritation.

"Son," the man said. "Is it all right if I call you that?"

"I'd rather you didn't."

"That's exactly what I'm talking about," Ma Stone said. "Always speaking his mind. Refuses to get down to his writing assignment."

"Patch, you can't get involved in other people's business."

So that was it. "I was worried about the girl." He couldn't stay away, not after what had happened to Jenny. "I just wanted to find out how she was doing. I've been praying for her every day."

The woman's eyes flashed. "And I suppose you think that makes you more spiritual than me?"

Patch looked away. Everything he said seemed to be taken wrong. "All Christians are supposed to pray."

"'Round here, people mind their own business. We don't want to draw any more WPA attention than necessary."

Good point. But Patch had the sense that something was very wrong with the townspeople here. Their faith seemed so twisted. Surely that wasn't how God wanted his people to behave—as though fate had a bigger role than he did and if they just kept quiet life would be easy.

How could they leave an injured child in the street?

Still, Patch forced himself to cool down, to think. He understood the risk Ma Stone and her husband were taking. If the police weren't fellow Christians, he was sure the WPA would already have been called.

When he thought about it, he realized how ungrateful he'd been.

"Your home, your rules," he said. "I'm sorry, ma'am. I haven't been very respectful. Would you forgive me?"

He could see she was flustered. But after a moment's thought she shook her head. "God gives second chances, and so do I."

So for the rest of the week Patch stayed out of the way. He spent the time praying for the little girl in the car accident but made no further attempt to find out how she was doing. He'd gotten in enough trouble already. In a way his foster family was right: she was in God's hands.

He wished he could feel better about his relationship with the Stones. But regardless of Mrs. Stone's words about second chances, things were not going well. He wondered if he should try living someplace different. But the few times he'd brought it up, Ma and Pa Stone wouldn't hear of it. That morning he'd asked again if this was a permanent arrangement. As with the other times, all they said was that it was God's will he come live with them.

"Thanks." It was all he could think to say.

He sighed and thought again of that little girl in the hospital. Which made him think again of Jenny.

He remembered the night at the Parkway Mall when he lay alone, slumped inside a sleeping bag while his family attended church. Though he was much better now, back then his stomach had hurt from ulcers, and they'd kept him in bed that day. How many times since then had he wished he'd gone to church with the others.

Of course, if he had, he might have died too.

God, why am I here?

He had no idea.

T*HAT'S MY BOY*, thought the Shining One.

The poor kid never quite seemed to have the picture in focus. He was always a step behind when it came to figuring out what God wanted.

Of course he couldn't blame the boy. He was only human.

Still, the angel wondered how Patch could have seen miracles, watched prayers being answered before his eyes, and still be so clueless. Faith was indeed quite fragile. Hadn't the guy watched a sky full of demons be chased back to hell? Hadn't he escaped McCry's claws when everything seemed desperate? And still he wondered—and worried.

That's what amused the Shining One so much. Didn't the boy see that if it was God's will for him to write an essay, he'd best comply? Even if the idea came from confused folks like the Stones.

16

PATCH HAD BEEN thinking. Even though he'd been writing, he knew he had to convince the Stones that the contest was a trap. But he knew they were after the prize money and were therefore unwilling to listen to reason.

"The prayer foundation has been poured," Ma Stone said, humming. "This is God's will. You will enter." She put her hand on Patch's desk. "And win."

"But it's like printing my location in the newspaper. Don't you know they're after me?"

"This isn't about you, Patch," Pa Stone said, opening a Bible. "You are to honor your father and mother. That's us now. You will obey."

"I've already called a remodeler. That's how strong my faith is." Ma Stone smiled at him.

It was hopeless. The way things were going he might as well call McCry and turn himself in.

He lost their attention suddenly. They stopped talking to Patch as the TV ad for rewards blared. Big promises that if they turned in a Christian they'd get a vacation to Hawaii. Sounded like something McCry was behind, just like the contest. She was always trying to buy loyalty.

Suddenly Patch's motivation to get that essay finished grew. He opened his document and got down to writing.

ERIN SMILED AT the sweet scene. Jenny sat in Erin's mom's lap in the bedroom, listening to a storybook. It used to be one of Erin's favorites. But Erin's smile faded as she listened now.

> *The beautiful mountains you see*
> *Evolved slowly for you and me.*
> *Man named the mountains, this is true.*
> *And that's far more than any "god" can do.*

Funny how the words came back. Erin must have heard that book hundreds of times growing up, listening to her mom's expressive voice, loving the pictures.

It was the first book she'd learned to read. *The End of God.*

She hated it now because the beautiful volume full of brilliant sunsets, majestic mountains, and wild animals taught that God didn't even exist. That he certainly didn't care enough to die for everyone's sins and come back to life as the Bible said Jesus had.

As a child, Erin had believed every word. She hadn't even thought twice about it, because her mom and dad told her so. *The End of God* had kept her from even considering that Someone out there might love her. God was a fairy tale.

Now Mrs. Morgan was turning Jenny from the truth. And the child lapped up the attention.

Erin waved to get Jenny's attention, but the little girl shushed her by putting her finger to her lips. She clearly wanted to hear the rest of the story.

"Mom, can I talk to you, please?"

The look she got scared her. "When we're through."

"No, right now." Erin wanted to see how far she could go.

"In a minute!"

Back to reading, her mom's voice mewed soft as a kitten. Jenny grinned. Erin gagged.

When her mom finished, she rose, grabbed Erin's elbow, and pulled her out of the bedroom.

Erin stifled a moan.

"I know what this is about," her mother said.

"You can't do it, Mom." Erin wasn't used to standing up to her, but she had to try. "Don't try to manipulate Jenny into thinking the way you do."

"But it's okay for you to manipulate her to think like you?"

"The difference is that I'm right," Erin said.

"You're deluded."

With a sneer, Mrs. Morgan returned to Jenny and the book.

Erin needed help. She couldn't stand alone in this. She needed a Bible and friends who agreed with her.

She needed hope.

WHY COULDN'T HE let go? Probably because the injured girl reminded Patch of Jenny. That's why he'd had so much trouble getting her out of his mind. If Jenny was hurt he would want as many people praying for her as possible, visiting her, caring for her. And since it was too late to do anything for his sister, it made him feel better to keep track of the child in the hospital.

He had to find out what was happening to her. How else could he pray effectively? The Stones wouldn't have to know. Not if he was careful.

The next day after school, when Ma Stone drifted off watching TV, Patch jumped on a borrowed bike and headed to the hospital. Even though he'd promised not to, he felt like going there was exactly what he was supposed to do.

At the information desk inside the main entrance, monstrous flower photos lined the wall. An old lady with reddish cheeks and curly white hair smiled at him, squinting through her glasses.

"A little girl in here was hit by car," he said carefully.

"Wasn't that sad?"

"I, ah, heard she was getting better."

The lady stood with obvious effort and leaned over the counter. "Are you making fun of me?"

Patch had no idea what she was talking about. "I didn't mean to." What had he done this time?

"I took time off yesterday afternoon to go to her funeral. It wasn't God's will that she be healed."

"No . . ." Feeling like he was going to be sick, Patch ran out, jumped on the bike, and started pedaling. He hadn't been able to save Jenny, and now, because he'd done nothing, another little girl was dead.

God, why are you doing this? What am I supposed to do?

17

SCHOOL WASN'T SO bad, really. But it was different being ignored by everyone, realizing that you were considered strange by the other students.

Oh, God, how I need you. Sometimes I'm just not sure you are listening.

Molly stopped typing and massaged an ache at her temple.

I have come from darkness to light. I have seen your power. I know your strength.

She hit Save and sat back in frustration. Why was writing this essay so complicated? Maybe because she wanted to say everything just right.

For a moment she thought back, remembered the time she'd spent at Demon's Bluff. Talk about a wild ride. She had hung tight to a flailing demon's tail. God had been with her.

But she wanted more. She wasn't interested in experiencing God only emotionally and in times of danger. She wanted to understand more about him, really know him. Like Patch and Jarrod. They had memorized Bible verses, used Scripture all the time.

That was her problem. Molly needed a Bible she could read for herself. Not just a page here and there. She still had the pages Patch had pulled from a Bible to send her notes when they were at New Peace Clinic together. She'd saved them like hidden treasures and almost worn them out. But she wanted more.

The question was how? It was illegal to own one. You needed an educational permit signed by a teacher to even look at the banned book. That's what Nancy had done for her art project last year. She cut faces from Scripture to decorate a mobile.

Nancy. Maybe she'd kept the parts of the Bible she hadn't shredded. It was worth a try.

SHE'S DEAD!" PATCH yelled. "Why didn't you tell me?" He had just returned from the hospital. The three of them sat in the cramped living room. He heard a Stones CD playing through the speakers.

"You had no right to know," Ma Stone said, face red with rage. "How did you find out?"

Her husband appeared calm, but Patch knew it was just a show. Although the man's voice remained soft, his cheeks flamed. "We warned you. You cannot disobey your parents without finding yourself in trouble."

"You are *not* my parents," Patch said evenly. Sure, they had given him a place to stay and food, but they were starving his soul.

"House arrest is our only choice," Pa Stone said. "You've got to be secluded from everyone else so you won't be a bad influence."

His wife patted her forehead with a tissue. "It is God's will. There's nothing we can do." She sniffled. "After all we've done for you."

Pa Stone dialed a number, and within minutes the police arrived and fitted Patch with a hard plastic strap clamped around his ankle. They set up a box with blinking lights on the fridge, and explained that if he left the house the transmitter alarm would go off.

A painful alarm.

Patch was in invisible chains. He could look at Seclusion Point in the backyard, but wasn't allowed to go that far. He was strictly an indoor kid until further notice.

How could this be happening when he had done nothing worse than inquire about a dying child?

ANOTHER BAD DAY.

Ever since Horrible Hope had started hanging around Granger, he'd hardly spoken to Nancy. Because of Hope, Nancy never had Granger alone. Hardly even saw him. Any time she tried to talk to him, Hope was there, smirking. Nancy saw darkness in the girl's eyes.

Her boyfriend was under Hope's spell.

It was outrageous. And it hurt. Nancy was the one who had stood up for Granger when no one else would. They'd been through a lot together. She'd even betrayed her new friends for him. She should be reaping the benefits.

She fumed. Then she decided to do something about it. She picked up the phone and called Marty. "Thought I was supposed to get some recognition."

Marty spoke up, "McCry wants to thank you in person." He chuckled. "You don't think I'd let you go unnoticed, do you?"

Nancy didn't like the way his words sounded. Like honey. Sticky. But she decided to trust him. A personal show of gratitude might make up for some of the humiliation caused by Hope's competition.

Surely Granger must care for Nancy. He had to. He had stood up to a raging demon to save her. This thing with Hope was temporary. Maybe even part of some plan of his.

Nancy hoped with all her heart it was true. Didn't he see that she was willing to give up anything for him? That she had? She'd lost her friends; they obviously didn't like hanging around her anymore.

She was confused. And Granger appeared to be too. Once upon a time he had claimed to be a Christian. Now he seemed repulsed by the very idea. Nancy wondered what had changed and what he believed.

That stupid ring was the trouble. He wouldn't let it go. Instead he'd figured out how to put it on or take it off whenever he wanted. He even thought he could control the power.

No way.

Nancy knew what that ring could make a person do, the horrible things it had communicated to her. She'd turned nasty under its powerful influence. Sure, with it she had been able to see into others' minds. But sometimes a person didn't want to know what lurked there.

She had to persuade Granger to get rid of the ring. Then maybe Hope's interest would wane as well.

But how? She had struggled to get rid of hers. Only one thing had worked.

Prayer.

Would God listen to her after all this time?

18

BARRY LIKED THE WPA kitchen. Fresh steaming mocha, plenty of cream, plus chocolate sprinkles. McCry had made him feel welcome. She had even issued him a WPA car.

"Think you could drop me off at my house?" Marty said, poking his head into Barry's office.

The guy couldn't stand him, yet still he had asked a favor. Barry respected that. But not too much.

"Bus not running today?" Barry opened the lid and blew. He knew that's what people did. But in truth, his coffee could never be too hot.

Marty pulled the door shut. "I know what you're trying to do."

"No time to chat. McCry has me on a very important project." Barry rose and tried to push past Marty.

Marty shoved back. "That was supposed to be mine."

Barry shrugged. "She found someone better for the job." He slammed Marty into the wall. "Stronger than I look, aren't I?"

He laughed as Marty rushed out, straightening his clothes and obviously hoping no one had heard the thump coming from Barry's office. Marty ran straight into McCry.

"Glad I caught you, Marty." McCry was in a hurry.

Her face looked grim, as always.

Marty brightened immediately, and Barry knew he hoped she had a juicy undercover assignment for him. Perhaps checking out a treasonous teacher or conducting a locker room search or some other school-related task. Small potatoes as far as Barry was concerned.

McCry smiled. "I want you to attend your classes full-time. You're dismissed for today."

With no further instruction, she brushed past him into Barry's office. Barry grinned and shut the door in Marty's face.

THE FIRST WEEK under house arrest was horrible. Patch hated it more than living underground. He had no say anymore. Ma and Pa Stone made all his decisions. He was stuck in the house with them unless she wandered outside to sit on her bench and stare at the sun-flowers. Patch didn't know what Pa Stone did in town, but when they were both gone, he felt terribly lonely.

All his teachers dropped off textbooks and assignments. The Stones were his go-betweens for school. Worse still, they selected books from the Sticklerville Library for him. Never any movies. And worst, the Stones played their music from morning till bedtime. Always and only their music. Patch had memorized all the songs. Tight harmonies, happy voices, but he knew the people behind the album covers. Who they really were. He had to say one thing for them: they certainly loved to perform. Did it all the time.

But he was trapped. He couldn't call the Tat Rats on the land line, couldn't run. Someone was always watching him, so he hardly had the chance to pull out his cell phone. Maybe later, but he'd have to be careful. One step outside would set off an alarm. Not an option. One wrong move and the police would call the WPA. Though Christians, they wouldn't give up their jobs for the likes of him. Pa

Stone said so. Patch figured that was why they were willing to help the Stones out by strapping the plastic ankle chains on Patch. If they got too annoyed with him they'd have him ready for McCry.

Patch tried to work on his essay, but he faced big-time writer's block. He'd already written and thrown away several versions. He knew what he had to do. Just put his fingers on the keyboard and type. Get something down and then edit like crazy.

He looked into the yard. At Ma Stone's Seclusion Point. The sunflowers were getting taller. If only he could step outside, stretch his legs. Sit on that bench for a minute. He longed to find a place to hide and pray.

As it was he felt pushed around by others, never in control. He hated the feeling.

If only Patch could think of an angle for the essay. Not that he expected to be the winner, but if he was, maybe the Stones would give him another chance—take off the anklet so he'd have a chance to sneak away.

"Give me something," he prayed. "Anything."

The toughest part of leading people to Christ was getting them to accept that they were sinners. No one even liked the word. But everyone sinned. That's why they needed God. Patch closed his eyes and imagined a kid like himself wearing a jacket many sizes too large for him, drooping to the floor. It was covered with pockets, each filled with too many pennies to count . . .

Patch wrote as fast as he could, telling how the pennies got there. The teen had put them there himself, one coin at a time. Though they weighed him down, he hardly noticed, because added a little at a time, the weight seemed normal. And the reward seemed worth it.

He liked the concept. This was a perfect picture of how sin could drag a person down before they even realized it.

He kept going, writing that the pockets now contained other coins as well, some gold, some silver. Those represented the good things people did. But even those noble efforts could bring a guy down if he became so obsessed with them that he forgot they couldn't save him from his sins.

Patch sat back. This could work.

19

Erin wondered how Patch was doing. She wished they could talk. Wished she could tell him about Jenny.

Which reminded her—she had something important to discuss with Patch's little sister.

She found the girl in her room and spoke without preamble.

"God is real, Jenny. He loves you."

With a frown, Jenny rolled off the bed, her feet thumping the floor. "Then why did he let my family die?"

Erin wasn't very good at coming up with comforting answers. She wished she had someone to talk to. For now she would just change the subject.

"Want to read *Winnie the Pooh*?"

Jenny climbed into Erin's lap. The girl was so innocent.

How did you explain God to a child? She could tell Jenny her brother was alive and that he loved her. But would she believe that until Patch held her in his arms?

In Jenny, Erin saw herself as a child. Trusting. Believing whatever anyone told her. Even if it wasn't the truth.

Her mom did not know the truth, so how could she pass it along? Pretty sad situation.

Only God could change Mrs. Morgan's heart. No amount of ranting would. But how could she pray for a woman who invited demons into the house?

When Erin's tears came, Jenny climbed down and went for a tissue. "What's wrong?"

"We need to pray," Erin said.

The child crept closer. "Are we allowed to?" she whispered.

Erin took Jenny's hand and closed her eyes. "Lord, please help Mom, Dad, and Terry to know your love like Jenny and I do."

Silently, she added, *And please let me find Jenny's brother.*

MOLLY FELT STRANGE standing at Nancy's front door. Nancy's mom barely cracked it open.

"What do you want?"

"Is Nancy home?"

The woman glowered at her. "She can't be bothered."

Molly could only recall the stories that had been told about her. That she never let Nancy do anything she wanted. That she made all of Nancy's decisions and didn't trust that her daughter could even pick out her own clothes.

From inside she heard Nancy's tired voice. "Who is it?"

Nancy's mom again: "I won't have her in this house. Talk to her on the porch."

Nancy came out and shut the door, but Molly was sure her mother was listening. Too bad. No more hiding the truth. "Do you know where I can get a Bible?"

Nancy's face turned white. She spun and rushed back inside, slamming the door.

Molly took that as a no.

Mom, could you take me to WPA headquarters?" Nancy looked down. "I'm supposed to pick up some award." She felt queasy. How could she be excited about turning her friends over to the authorities? What kind of a person was she?

Her mother's eyes sparkled and she clapped her hands. "At last, my little girl's getting the recognition she deserves."

"It's no big deal. Just a gift certificate or something."

I'm making a huge mistake, aren't I, God?

Nothing. No answer, no whisper. Just as she suspected. He wasn't willing to have anything to do with her.

"Congratulations." Nancy's mom patted her on the shoulder.

Yeah, great, Nancy thought. The distraction might help her forget the sad shock she saw on Molly's face when she'd refused her the Bible.

Claudia wasn't much of a cook, but her mom had been working a lot lately. Dinner consisted of rice, spice, and black beans. Claudia went all out and folded the blue paper napkins in half. It looked nicer that way.

"Delicious," her mom said, closing her eyes.

Claudia wondered if she was about to fall asleep.

"Tough day at the office?"

Her mom chewed slowly. "Some people at work . . . You wouldn't believe what they're saying about your cult. It's tough defending you." She took another bite. "But I stick up for you even though everyone makes fun of me." Her voice sounded sad. "You're still my little girl, and I love you."

Claudia slipped from her chair. She bent and hugged her mom, listening to her sobs.

"Jesus does love us." Sometimes even Claudia wasn't exactly sure what that really meant. God seemed abstract when people started acting mean.

"Who is he?"

Was her mom really wondering?

"Why would he give a rip about someone like me?"

Claudia saw the open door and stepped through. "He's the Savior of the world. God's son. He died for our sins."

"I've made plenty of mistakes. But does that make me a sinner?"

Her mom looked into her eyes and Claudia felt the roles reverse. She was the parent trying to assure the confused child. Trying to give hope.

"We all are."

After she told her mom the basics about Jesus, she went to her room to think. And to give her mother time to do the same.

She was worried. Who had been spreading the word about the Christ-Kids? Someone was talking and the number of suspects was quite limited. If the adults at Mom's job knew, but the others at school had no idea, it must be McCry.

But who had blabbed to McCry?

Erin? Molly? No way.

Nancy? Had to be. She still wanted to get on Granger's good side. And maybe turning in her friends would help somehow.

Claudia wanted to scream at the girl for ruining their plans.

Instead she prayed.

20

YOU'RE RIGHT, SWEETUMS. He might be God's special delivery for us. The reward we've been waiting for." Pa Stone spoke in his rumbly voice on the other side of the bedroom door, obviously wanting Patch to hear.

"Maybe we'll have a little extra for some new dresses." Ma Stone sounded as though she had a megaphone.

"If it's God's will, there's nothing that boy can do but obey. And that money's as good as ours."

The two of them tromped away. They'd gotten their point across. These days, since they'd made it clear what his assignment was, the Stones left him to his work. They called him to meals, but didn't talk much. They came and went, back and forth to work and church. Patch stayed behind. When he was alone he couldn't help wondering if the sensors actually worked. If he walked out, would anyone really come running? He wanted to find out, but he was afraid.

Tonight he worked on his essay. English wasn't his favorite subject, but creative writing was fun once he got started. After a while, though, his knees ached from sitting. So did his shoulders and neck. He stretched in the doorway.

A few hours later, Patch emerged to sniff out a snack. He didn't mean to listen in. But they still didn't seem used to having him around.

"Cancer?" Pa Stone said. "They're sure?"

His wife's voice shook. "I'm supposed to die." She sounded like a dove, quiet and sad. Nothing like the booming voice he'd heard outside his door earlier that day.

"Only if it's God's will."

A chill ran down Patch's spine. Surely she would get treatment. Though she wasn't much more than a stranger to him, he didn't want her to be sick. He wouldn't wish that on anybody. And she shouldn't give up either.

Why weren't they praying about it?

She was sniffling. Pa Stone said, "Heaven's only a heartbeat away."

Guess that was his idea of comfort. They would just wait for the inevitable.

"Can I pick any songs I want for the funeral?" Patch had an idea the music would be from *The Stones Sing Their Favorites* album. She'd been playing that one a lot lately.

"Choose the food and the flowers too," he said.

Patch pulled his door closed. How could they just give up?

God's will?

No way God wanted his people to give in so easily. Patch decided to do something about it.

Call it an experiment.

"Dear God, please heal Ma Stone. Keep her around singing for a long time."

Maybe a miracle would change their minds.

JARROD HAD PASSED along the information. Next to his bedroom window, Patch slipped his cell phone out and dialed the number, excited. With any luck, he might be talking to Erin on the phone soon.

"Hello, Erin here."

Patch felt a swell of emotion. She sounded so close.

"Hey, whoever you are, you'd better say something or I'm hanging up!"

"It's me."

"P—" She stopped herself before saying his name.

"Can't tell you where I am, but I got the message."

"That's right. You left a package behind. An important one." Erin's voice sounded strong.

"A package?" He had no idea what she was talking about, but he knew this call could be monitored. It's wasn't safe for either of them. No details allowed.

"I'll try to get there."

"You have to." Her voice sounded agitated. He could tell it meant a lot to her for him to come.

Patch felt the ring in his pocket. "I've got something for you too."

Erin passed along a private e-mail address.

AFTER HEARING HIS voice, Erin made more plans. What if Patch couldn't make it to her? Then she needed to find a way to get to him. Rescue Jenny and reunite them. She had to.

At least she knew he was alive. Of course she understood why he couldn't say much, and why he couldn't provide directions to his hiding place. So she'd have to try a different route.

Nancy was her closest association with the WPA crew. If she was on the inside, maybe Erin could squeeze her for some information. Yeah, the gang hadn't thought her "telephone" plan would work too well, but her options were limited. Nancy, Marty, Granger, McCry.

Erin called Nancy. "I need your help. Would you please see if Marty knows where Patch is? He might have heard something from McCry." The silence stretched. "It's important. Please, Nancy."

"You know, I've decided I'm not into the whole religious thing anymore." Nancy's voice sounded disinterested.

What was going on with this girl? "I know we can't talk a lot over the phone. Someone might turn us in."

"You got that right." Erin thought she heard Nancy chuckle.

"Well, couldn't you at least try to help me, help Patch?"

"Like you'd do the same for me."

"Of course."

"Forget it. I've got my own back to protect." Nancy hung up.

With a sigh, Erin prayed that God would help her friend. Then she worried about Nancy's comments. Did they mean Erin had gotten the gang into even more trouble? As usual, she was probably going about everything backward. But she had to try. Patch deserved to know about Jenny.

Erin's thoughts turned to her mom. Their relationship was in tatters. She treated Erin as though she was crazy. Never listened. Believed that only her own views mattered. Erin worried about her mom's eternal life—was she going to hell? Probably.

So what was Erin doing about it? Maybe talking to Mom about God wasn't the smartest thing at this point. Okay, so she should work things the other way around.

First, Erin should pray. Then pray some more.

As for the essay, she didn't feel like working on it. Didn't have time. Let Molly speak her piece, let Claudia write a winner. Words failed Erin. Right now it was more important to pray for her mom and be a good big sister to Jenny.

Happy endings were God's specialty, right?

UPDATE TIME. TWO demons having a heart-to-heart. Barry scarfed Mexican food, drenched with hot sauce. He splashed and crunched as he spoke to Hope.

"McCry and Marty are nowhere near catching Patch. McCry has resorted to bullying Erin for information and Marty is useless. Should I give him a ring? Even the playing field a little?" Conflict was always good.

Hope gave him a look. "He doesn't deserve one. Of course, they both might try harder with a little help from below."

"That's just what we need. More backup."

"No. We can handle this." Hope grabbed the edge of the table. "I want us to do what we came to do."

"All I want is Patch," Barry said. "I don't care who turns him in."

"You're cold," Hope said. "Almost like a real guy." She wiped his mask with a napkin.

Barry held up his hand and caught the waitress's attention. "Another order of sauce. Extra hot."

21

NANCY WATCHED GRANGER walk past her, craning his neck. He was obviously looking for Hope. *Stupid guy*, Nancy thought. Especially when he had someone who liked him right in front of him. Liked him enough that she'd even been praying about how to make it work with him.

Hadn't she already turned traitor to stay on Granger's good side? When she'd found out about him taping her friends, she offered to create a confession on her own. She did a lot of finger pointing to keep anyone from asking too many questions.

She thought about the scene at the WPA office. They'd given her a cheap "Service Rendered" certificate, signed with McCry's scrawl. Worthless. When she got home she'd showed her mom and then shoved it in a bottom dresser drawer with some other old junk. At least she'd gotten a twenty-five-dollar gift certificate to the bookstore. That made turning in her old pals okay.

Right?

No. She was horrible. What had she done?

She shook her thoughts away. *Get off the guilt*, she told herself. *Focus on Granger or you'll lose him.*

Weird or not, Nancy still cared about him, so why not let him know?

With a nod of determination, she set off down the hallway after Granger. He was at his locker, so she sidled up and tapped him on the shoulder. He turned quickly, but his face fell when he realized who it was.

"Probably dumb to say," Nancy said, "but I really like you."

Granger blinked. Then a small smile crept across his face.

"When Trevor tried to kill me, you fought." Nancy's heart beat faster. "I wanted you to know I care about you." She remembered the way he'd stood up for her when no one else could. He'd hurled rocks as the demon tried to crush her chest. A guy had to like a girl to do that. Had to.

She saw a look in his light-brown eyes and a sweetness in his smile that reminded her of the old Granger, the way he had been before he got the ring.

He hesitated. "Yeah, well, thanks, but I have to be honest. I don't feel the same way. All I can think about is Hope."

Nancy's face felt hot as she turned away. Granger put a hand on her shoulder.

"I still want to be friends," he said.

That was the last thing she wanted to hear. "Sure."

"You've met Hope," he said. "You think she'd like flowers or candy better?"

It couldn't get much worse than this. How could she convince him Hope was nothing more than a weasel with nice hair?

"Why ask me? Consult your stupid ring." She pointed at the shiny band.

"*Stupid*? I'll bet you wish you still had yours."

"Not on your life. I wanted to die when I had that ring on."

"Not me," he said. "It doesn't control me. It gives me the upper hand."

GRANGER FUMED AS he scoped out the cafeteria. Where had Hope gone? She'd better not be off getting friendly with someone else. He was starting to feel protective of her, like he used to about Nancy.

He thought of their conversation in the hallway earlier. What had he ever seen in her? Plain and boring. Nancy had been too scared to keep her ring. He wasn't. It gave him the inside track, knowing what people were thinking.

Unable to spot Hope, Granger hit the locker room and slipped on a ragged T-shirt and his sweats. A run sounded good. Anything to keep his mind from wondering where Hope was . . . and who she might be with.

He hightailed it around the oval two, three, four times, panting. Then he realized someone was chasing him. For a moment he thought he was back in the desert, a demon breathing down his neck. He glanced back and slowed. Marty.

"What's up?" Granger didn't hide his irritation. Couldn't he ever have a little peace?

Marty jumped right into his favorite topic. "I hate Barry. I really do."

"The new WPA star?" Hey, at least the discussion wasn't about himself. Granger wanted to keep it that way. "What are you going to do about it?"

But Granger already knew because of the ring.

"I need some inside information on him. You can help."

"Maybe I can," Granger said. "We're friends." Marty was dumb enough to believe that.

They walked to the center of the track where no one could hear them.

"Watch," Granger said. Then he spoke to the ring. "Tell me about Barry." He watched Marty's face. "Great guy," he said, repeating the voice in his head.

"That ring's a piece of junk."

"There's more, Marty. It says to keep your eye on Hope. The two are closer than they seem."

"Wonder what that means."

Granger had no idea, but he didn't like it. Hope and Barry? Not good news.

"I see them together a lot," Marty said. "Hope's even shown up at the office to have lunch with Barry."

So much for my faithful Hope, Granger thought.

Marty wouldn't believe him, but Granger wondered if Barry could be like Trevor, a demon in disguise.

Taking a chance, he asked the question. Out loud.

Marty looked at him like he was crazy. "You kidding me, man? Don't tell me you're starting up that crazy stuff again." He smirked.

Granger felt like punching him. The guy had no idea what was going on, because he'd missed the spectacle at Demon's Bluff.

"The ring said yes."

"So now your magic ring's telling you it can reveal demons?"

Among other things. Granger wasn't sure himself what all the ring could do. "Look, Marty." Granger held it between his thumb and forefinger and peered at Marty through it as if through a telescope. "You're currently demon free." He lowered the ring and wondered what would happen if he asked the ring to reveal the real Marty, the guy behind the WPA jock persona. It might be interesting—something he could use against Marty later. Maybe he'd try it another time.

"Impressive. Really convincing." Marty looked bored.

"The masks they use are scary, they're so normal. Trevor actually looked like a cool guy. But beneath, he was a monster."

"Fine. Look, I've got to go by headquarters. If you take me, we can check Barry out. He's always there."

That was fine with Granger. They'd confront Barry, find out once and for all if he hailed from hell or somewhere farther north.

THINGS WERE CHANGING. Patch could feel it. Last night, unable to go anywhere or do anything, Patch had swept the kitchen, set the table, and made a salad, all without being asked. Ma and Pa Stone were amazed and appreciative. They sang some songs after supper. Patch even joined in.

Truth was, every time Patch thought of the woman he prayed.

"Not a bad meal, son."

Patch had nodded, wishing he could remind this man that he was not his father.

"Would you like more coffee?" Patch said.

The woman tapped her cup. Patch poured.

"Ma Stone and I have been talking," Pa Stone said. "You seem to be turning over a new leaf. We've decided to let you out of the house to get some exercise."

They'd said they would get the police to calibrate the device so Patch could go to the edge of the yard. Seclusion Point would be back in bounds, but one step into the street out front and the alarm would go off.

"This is temporary," Ma Stone said, sounding tired. "It all depends on how well you follow instructions."

Patch had been elated. He said a polite good night and went to his room, where he sat at the computer. Inspired, he opened his essay document and typed: "The boy's pockets were full, so he bought some bags and tied them to his belt and filled them too."

The world's worries, he thought. *All our pains and cares.*

Today, anklet calibration changed, Patch walked along the grass he'd mowed that morning, enjoying a little freedom for the first time in a long time. He watched the flashing green light on his leg. If it turned red, that was bad.

A familiar boy raced by on his bike. He looked sad.

"Nice wheels!" Patch called out.

The boy buzzed another circle and slammed his brakes. He was the one whose sister had died. A fuzzy monkey hung around his neck, furry arms sewn together.

"I shouldn't talk to you," the boy said, sounding scared.

"My sister died too. You miss her, don't you?"

The boy's face wrinkled. "I didn't mean to hurt her."

"It was an accident, I know. I was there."

The boy raced away.

22

MOLLY WAS STILL thinking of her meeting with Nancy a couple of days ago. Mostly because she felt sorry for her. She'd looked miserable—and those clothes she was wearing. Whew. No wonder the girl didn't get out much.

Wow. What a mean, petty thought.

Something else worried her, though. Seriously. What was Nancy hiding? If she still had a Bible, Molly hoped the girl would pull it out and start reading. But Molly had to find a copy of her own. Patch had once told her people used to have many Bibles. More than one per person. Now they were a rarity, nearly impossible to find.

She'd have to look online. Students supposedly had complete access to anything they wanted to check out on the Web. But she had to wonder if someone might secretly be tracking her every keystroke. So far, no problem. But this was different.

At the computer lab at school, Molly entered her student ID number and logged onto the Web. Several editions of the Bible were for sale, but they were very expensive.

Then she found the free stuff. "Bible studies."

All she'd had to do was look. Most of the churches in town had been converted to museums or movie theaters. But she found a remnant of believers online. It helped to know a battalion of believers had your back.

One blog hit her heart. A girl wrote about wanting to learn more face to face. Molly typed an encouraging note.

On another blog she found a post from a Patch Meister. Couldn't be him, could it?

She shot back a message mentioning the first page of Scripture Patch had ever smuggled to her at the New Peace Clinic. She used a screen name no one but the real Patch would know.

Maybe she'd make a secret new friend.

Or find a faithful old one.

Hope WAS IN a bad mood. She'd been doing exactly what she'd practiced, what Flabbygums had said any demon could do if they were having trouble. She'd made a devil-to-devil call home on the telepathic hell-line. Basically a help desk for demons.

So far, though, Hope was having trouble. Her help demon was waffling, refusing to give her any concrete advice. How dare the thing defy her?

She concentrated on thought messaging as she strolled through the city park. The connection was crystal clear. But she didn't like what she heard.

Granger discovered he could use his ring to identify us as demons?

How could those in charge be so brainless? It would be embarrassing for Barry to be found out and sent back to the minors. Wasn't going to happen to her though.

I'm going to be invisible to his ring. Got that?

Hope heard the response and felt her demon form expanding, threatening to burst from her skin.

Granger knows Barry's connected to me?

It was unbelievable. This hell-line wasn't any help. The demon on the other end was only interested in howling with laughter as it relayed more and more bad news. Hope needed to make her case to somebody with more experience.

Put your supervisor on!

But the demon on the other end refused. Now it was chewing her out! Hope felt like puking.

Her final plea: *Can't you help me work this out?*

The voice called her a teen beauty queen.

Okay, fine, so she didn't exactly look like a powerful demon in her current disguise. But that didn't mean she couldn't take care of business. She just had to prove herself. And the best way to do that? Easy.

Get Patch.

Y OU CAN'T FOOL me," Erin's mom said, hands on her hips. Her blue dress matched her eyes.

As usual, Erin had no idea what her mother was talking about. She'd been keeping a low profile. Doing her schoolwork and keeping up with chores, helping out with Terry and Jenny. If she could have picked a day in which she might've squeezed out a compliment from her mom, today would be it.

"I know exactly what you're doing. McCry warned me."

Of course, add McCry to any mix, and any loaf is bound to flop. "I'm trying to be obedient, Mom."

"'Loving me into the kingdom,'" Mrs. Morgan said, thick with sarcasm. "McCry said you'd try. It won't work. You can't fool me. You can pretend you've changed, but I know what you're really like. I know the real you."

So did Erin. In a way, her mother was right. "But I'm different now, Mom. Don't you believe people can change?"

"Some, maybe, but not you. I know you too well. And if I catch you telling Jenny any more of those Bible myths, McCry will hear about it."

Threats. Who was Erin supposed to obey?

God or Mom?

23

SECLUSION POINT. BRIGHT yellow sunflowers pushed toward the fence line. It felt great to have some space to wander in. Patch settled onto the bench in the corner flower garden and thanked God for giving him a moment of peace. Hey, it wasn't Hawaii, but at least being kept under house arrest meant that he was staying out of trouble.

But soon the taste of freedom turned to frustration. Patch could walk along the sidewalk, which was great. He could go even farther than he thought he might, and still no flashing red showed on his transmitter. But what would happen if he stepped into the street?

The thought came to him: maybe he was free to find his friends and didn't know it.

He'd seen other kids walking the streets. But they didn't say a word. Clearly, they'd been warned.

Except that little boy, who'd finally told Patch his name was Ned. He was Patch's only friend, although he was so young he went to school half days. They didn't talk about his sister much, but he did tell Patch his favorite toy was a stuffed monkey named Gilla she had given him. Other than that they discussed two things: his bike and baseball. He wanted to play in the big leagues someday. Go to college on a sports scholarship.

Big plans for such a little guy.

"Dad says it's God's will," the boy had said earlier today.

That again. What did it really mean? The two of them sat on the front steps.

"So you're doing a lot of practicing?"

The boy got up and assumed a hitter's stance. "Not bad, huh?"

"Looks good. Bring your back elbow up." Patch stood behind the boy and adjusted his feet.

Suddenly Ned turned. "Where's my sister? Tell the truth."

The question surprised Patch. "In heaven with Jesus. I believe that."

"Why did she have to die? I miss her."

Patch felt the same about Jenny.

"I don't know, Ned." Why hadn't Ned's parents done more to save her? He certainly couldn't explain it.

With his face twisting, Ned sped away, skinny legs churning.

Patch missed that freedom.

THEY FIRED ME, Claudia," her mother said. "Cheryl McCry forced them to because of you. That's what my boss said."

No job, no money. Where would they get food? How would they pay the rent?

All because of her.

Oh, God. Please help us. It was all she could think to pray.

"I'm sorry, Mom," she said, trying to embrace the woman.

But her mother wouldn't have it. "I know you say you have faith in God," she said, shaking. "Don't you see what it's cost us? They even refused to write a letter of recommendation."

"God knows. He'll watch over us."

"Hope he can pay our bills." Her mother trudged to the kitchen.

What could Claudia do? The odds seemed terrible, but in a way the contest was her only hope. If she could win, maybe the government would loosen up on believers and those they cared about. Those like her.

But would she have time? And could she win?

She buckled down. Wrote about her mom. About how people thought God only loved them if everything was going great. This essay gave her a chance to speak her mind, to open her heart.

Maybe her essay would be her mom's answer to prayer.

Still . . . until the world became more open to Christians, the least Claudia could do was find a job. But what if word got out that she was a Christian? She thought a moment. She wouldn't have to worry if she could work somewhere where no one cared, a place where people were in their own little world. Possibly a restaurant where employees were regularly hired and fired.

24

THEY'D SNUCK OUT of school early. Marty said they wouldn't get in trouble. He and Granger parked at the WPA building. Marty signed in and the two were issued sticky nametags. They went up the elevator and down a long hallway, directly to Barry's office. Marty made a face.

"Even gets his name on the door," he said. "Yuck."

"Can hardly wait to meet him," Granger whispered.

Marty entered without knocking.

Barry looked up. "Thought I heard the ice cream truck. Better hurry. Little boys don't want to miss that."

Marty rounded the desk and yanked Barry from his seat. "You're a phony, and we can prove it."

Barry wrenched himself from Marty's grasp, straightened his mangled collar. "McCry will hear about this."

Granger held the ring in front of Barry's face—and saw.

Barry turned ashen. Granger guessed Demon Guy knew about the ring, what it could do.

"Get that away from me." Barry reached for a button on his desk.

"No calling security!" Marty said, slapping his hand away.

"Look," Granger said, staring into the heart of the ring at the face of a craggy old demon. Thick head, blinking lizard eyes. Caught in that tiny frame was a slobbering, toothy raptor, wings flapping. Snapping strips of what looked like human skin stretched across his face. Gross.

Granger got it. The ring captured Barry's transformation from fake human to genuine beast.

Marty peeked over Granger's shoulder. "Insane! I'll never doubt you again, man."

"Give me that!" Barry shrieked.

Granger fled, hearing a thump behind him as Marty momentarily held Barry off. All he could think about was Hope. Marty had said she and Barry were tight.

He had to tell Hope the truth. He didn't want Barry hurting her.

McCry PINCHED HERSELF, hard. Right under the armpit in a tender place that made her teeth clench. "You're getting soft." She looked into the mirror, saw her short gray hair standing at attention. And those beady silver eyes.

What had happened to her old scary self? She wanted children to fear her again. She'd gotten soft associating with Frazier. But the woman was gone and she was in charge. No more excuses.

The new plan was perfect. She knew exactly how to make school a living hell for those troublesome kids. They might not even get out alive. God lovers, warmongers. They were evil for refusing to go along with the Gospel of tolerance.

She'd called the head of the marketing department. He stood before her now, quaking.

"Stand up straight." She pushed a chair toward him. It scraped across the tile.

"What would you like, Ms. McCry?" His pen shook as he pressed his scratch pad.

"Posters. Big bright ones." She smiled. "Three varieties. One starring Claudia, one Molly, and one Erin, of course."

"Are we commending these teens?" The marketing man acted clueless.

"No. We're destroying their lives." McCry threw out words. "Liars. Cheaters. Traitors. Antihumanist." She flicked her hand. "You get the idea."

"More like WANTED posters."

She nodded. "But do a better job than the ones you created for Patrick Johnson. On these I want their faces to look perfect. Angelic. To inspire jealousy. I want these girls to be hated on sight."

The man slunk toward the door. "That all, ma'am?"

"I want them ready by morning." She waited for the whine.

"Impossible—" he started, then quickly shut up at the look on her face. "We'll take care of it for you."

"One more thing. Contact information. Be sure to include home address, phone number, cell, e-mail. We want them to know exactly how much their religious beliefs are despised in this modern world."

"They might be hurt." The man held the doorknob. "What about riots?"

"Let's let things sort themselves out."

The man left and McCry smiled. She loved the concept. Torture by the hands of classmates and friends.

The perfect reward for those who dared to try noncompliance.

Erin WANTED TO talk to someone, but her friendships were crumbling. Everybody had their own problems.

Chatting with Nancy was not an option. Her first loyalty was to Granger. And if Erin talked to her she'd have to endure more boring stories about how jealous she was of Hope.

Molly. A loveable A-1 weirdo. Always saying just what she thought without thinking. Erin admired her guts, but she was looking for some-body more grounded and tactful.

Claudia? She was an on-again, off-again friend. She seemed to have turned the corner, but Erin wasn't sure. And yet, the fact that her mom lost her job because of Claudia's faith made Erin wonder. That could impact the girl. Christ changed people. Even the Claw.

Claudia it was. She dialed her number.

"Hello?" Claudia sounded sad. When Erin asked why, Claudia explained her mom's work situation.

"What are we going to do?" Erin said. "There aren't many people we can trust."

"I don't see any middle ground."

"What do you mean?" Erin was worried. "Either let our faith flop like Nancy or go all out like Molly?"

"Mom's lost enough," Claudia said. "So have I."

"Guess you've made your choice. Can I pray for you?"

"Won't do any good."

Too bad. Erin intended to keep praying, keep hoping that Claudia would pull out of her slump.

25

WHY HAD HE agreed to this assignment?

McCry. Barry was ready to give her the title of honorary demon. She was driving him nuts, coming in his office every fifteen minutes asking about Patrick Johnson's whereabouts. She loved that word: *whereabouts*. Said it over and over.

And then yesterday's psycho encounter with Granger and his ring. Great. Now Granger and Marty knew the truth. Of course, would they have the mental capacity to accept what they saw without rationalizing it away? And anyway, who'd believe them?

Barry wasn't worried, just extremely peeved.

Finally there was good old Patch. Still hiding. When would he learn there was no place to run? Barry and Hope would find him. No doubt.

Maybe he'd made a mistake getting on Marty's bad side. They could have worked together. Less one-on-one time with McCry would have been good.

She stood across from his desk now. "We've got to find him."

"Can't tell you what I don't know." He'd hoped to get news from her. Humans were worthless. "You must have an idea. Some way to put pressure on him?"

The woman looked as if a bucket of water had been poured over her head. "I didn't want to do this, but it's time." She told him about Jenny.

What in the world? "You have his baby sister?" Barry couldn't believe this. "Don't you think it's time to use her?"

"She has no idea where he is," McCry said.

Maybe the woman was afraid the girl might get hurt. Fool. She couldn't be that soft.

"If Patch found out about her, he'd come running," Barry said.

McCry seemed to be weighing something in her mind. "She's a child."

"I'd never harm a child," Barry said. *If there was an adult around.* He was an equal opportunity tormentor. "Have you heard of OpenEyez.com?"

"Sure. The video site."

"How about we upload something about a lost little girl? I'll be the director. Eventually Patch will learn of it and come running."

McCry was easy. "You're in charge." She gave Barry Erin's address and issued him a camera from the supply room.

When she left, Barry unzipped his mask at the back, popped his desk stapler open, and used it to scratch his neck. Office supplies rocked.

Y OU'RE LIKE YOUR father." Nancy wasn't sure what her mom meant, but it certainly wasn't nice. "When you have a chance, you blow it."

"What do you mean?"

"Like Granger," her mom said. "Such a nice young man. So polite."

Nancy thought her mom disliked everybody.

"I still like him, Mom." *A lot, actually.*

"Of course you do. If only you'd smile. Boys are attracted to friendly girls. Maybe you should call him."

What had gotten into her?

"You won't stay with us forever, Nancy. Might be a good idea to develop some friends."

Mom was right. Nancy wished she had people she could count on. But she had betrayed her friends. And for nothing.

She regretted that now. Regretted helping Marty. Regretted how mean she'd been to Molly when her friend had come over. "I'm a little disconnected right now, Mom."

"Like your father."

Nancy walked to her quiet bedroom and switched on some classical music. She remembered the battles against Trevor. She'd been part of the gang back then. Pitched in and really helped.

Molly's question about finding a Bible had triggered a memory. Nancy had been terrified her parents might find what lurked in the bottom of her dresser drawer. Since returning from the clinic and then from Demon's Bluff, she'd never dared open it.

Maybe her mother was acting so strange because she'd located the Bible. She'd have to check.

When the time was right.

Erin saw a poster. *What in the world?* Molly's face stared down at her, three feet wide. There were words under it. Horrible words. They called others to "take action against the filthy God lovers." To tear the traitors from their midst. And more—much more and much worse.

She covered her mouth. Molly's personal contact information was on the poster. All of it. Even the creepiest kid in school could find her now. Poor girl. That's what happened when you pushed your beliefs too far.

Erin ripped the poster off the lamppost, then realized there were more on every post and building around. There were hundreds. Every blank space was plastered. A Halloween horror arriving a few weeks early.

And then Erin saw another face. Claudia. Same details. Same plea to do something about the filthy "christ-kids." They didn't even have the decency to capitalize Christ.

What was happening? Who was behind this?

McCry. Of course. Who else would be so vile? So unconcerned about the safety of her friends.

Or herself.

Erin saw the final version of the notice. With her picture front and center. She looked as if she could have stepped out of a women's magazine. Her hair was perfect, her skin flawless. She felt like tearing the poster in half.

The whole school knew. She couldn't hide her faith anymore.

She had one choice: reject Jesus . . .

Or face the consequences.

26

PATCH SAT BACK and read the final paragraph of his essay.

The boy could hardly put one foot in front of the other. His coat was full, every pocket and bag packed. And still he looked for more.

Was it as good as he thought?

Did he dare ask Ma Stone to read it? They were hardly close, but something had changed toward her in his heart. Whenever she came to mind, he prayed for God to heal her.

Now her scowls didn't dig as deep. Sometimes she even offered a kind word.

He went to find her. "Would you mind looking at this?"

The woman didn't fill the recliner like she once had. She sat up and adjusted the footrest on her chair.

"I need an objective opinion." He smiled. "I like it too much."

"Happy to help, Patch." She had never used his nickname before. Always "Patrick" or "young man."

Patch wanted to stay as she read but resisted the urge. Instead he wandered outside and found little Ned biking in big circles.

"We're moving," Ned said. "I'm going to miss you."

Patch was surprised. "Where are you going?"

"My dad says anywhere but here." Ned made a face and Patch imagined he was trying to copy his father.

"You're not sure where?"

Ned shook his head, pulled the front tire up in a wheelie. Patch cheered.

Ned's cell phone rang in his pocket. He slammed on his brakes and answered. Patch heard panic in his voice as he spoke, then ended the call.

"Gotta go, Patch." Tears tumbled. "Our house is on fire!"

MOLLY WAS BENT over the lab computer, shiny black hair in a rubber band. Erin watched.

How strange. She doesn't know I'm here. Erin crept closer. It wasn't nice, but she was curious.

When she saw what Molly was working on, Erin gasped. On the screen, in large letters, were the words "Bible Study."

Molly must have seen her reflection on the screen. She whacked a button and the screen went blank as she turned.

"Oh, it's just you," Molly said. "Why are you sneaking around? Grab a seat."

"You're the dangerous one," Erin said, rolling a chair next to Molly.

"Well, we don't have a church, do we?"

Erin shook her head.

"And we don't know what we're doing."

"Can't argue with that," Erin said. "Hey, have you seen these?"

Molly hardly glanced at the posters. "Yeah. Free advertising for Jesus." She clicked the mouse. "I love 'em."

"Aren't you afraid?" Since she'd spotted them, Erin had felt every eye was looking her way. She thought she heard people whispering.

Molly ignored her. "I found an awesome Web site a couple days ago."

"Aren't you afraid of getting caught?"

"I'm afraid I'm going to mess up and do something Jesus doesn't want me to do. Listen, there are lots of others like us. Believers." She lowered her voice. "Lots of people who completely trust God for everything. Let me show you."

"Fascinating. Or should I say incriminating."

Erin and Molly swung around.

McCry.

Busted.

27

THE HELP WANTED sign in the coffee shop window could be Claudia's caffeinated answer to prayer. She went up to the man behind the counter.

"What'll you have?"

"A new career," Claudia said and smiled. So did the guy. He had short hair, not quite buzzed. Kind of handsome, actually.

"Who do I talk to about a job?"

"Me. Name's Bill."

They sat at a round table.

"What's your favorite coffee?" Bill said.

"I don't drink the stuff unless I have to," Claudia said. "But I have friends who love it. And my mom's favorite is Kona."

Bill stuck out his hand. "I'm not looking for an expert; I'm looking for personality, and you've got it. You're hired. You can learn the potions."

Claudia wasn't really looking for a career. She would work her hours, collect her check. And when she'd made enough, she'd leave. Her goal was to help provide for her family. That way her mom wouldn't have to admit to anyone else that her daughter had turned into a Christ-Kid. Claudia needed to think about someone other than herself.

If she took this step, maybe her mom would decide to change too. Trust more, worry less.

Hey, it could happen. Probably her hope came from the fact that Erin was praying for her. And she'd been sending up her own prayers like arrows in the night. Just because she had a setback, she'd decided, she couldn't give up.

That's what the old Claudia would have done.

Whatever she did, Claudia knew she needed to be consistent. No wavering. That was the only way her mom might see that she was serious about her faith.

BEING IN THE wrong place at the right time was Hope's specialty. She watched Claudia scurry behind the waist-high wooden counter. The girl's blond hair was pasted to her temples. Those long, painted nails wouldn't last long on this job.

Hope laughed.

Fool. Young human minds opened up to any lame idea. Good thing only a few had learned to think first and act second. And Hope had a plan, a way to destroy Claudia's hopes and dreams for herself—and her mother.

This was going to be a great day.

Hope sat watching people flow in and out. The manager wiped tables near her. She offered her best smile and planted a thought in his mind. Guys were so lame. They often acted on the first idea that skittered across their brains.

"Been nursing that latte for quite a while," he said. "Want a fresh one?" Hope knew Claudia was watching.

"I'm kind of hungry."

"Cookie? Brownie? Muffin?"

"Make any by hand?" She spun him like a top.

"I'll pick out one for you." He leaned in next to her ear. "On the house."

Hope basked in Claudia's glare. She could see that Bill was like all the rest—incapable of resisting her. Barry might say it was all because of her realistic costume, but Hope knew otherwise. She was an actress to rival the screen greats.

He handed an oatmeal raisin cookie to Claudia and asked her to deliver it. She stomped to the table and slapped it down, the plate clattering. Hope considered complaining but took a different approach. As Claudia headed back to the counter, Hope said, "More cream, please?"

Claudia paused. Bill was watching. She turned and pointed.

"Right over there."

"You're doing a good job," Hope said.

"Thanks," Claudia grumped.

"Wish *I* could make a little extra money."

Claudia raised her eyebrows at Bill. He shrugged. She pulled up a chair at Hope's table.

"Haven't I seen you in school?"

"Only when I can't avoid it." Hope smiled. "School, I mean. Not you."

Claudia laughed. "They'll probably have an opening within a few weeks."

"Who'd give up a job like this?" Hope said.

"I'm not planning on staying long," Claudia said, her blue eyes bright. "I'll put in a good word for you."

"Why so short-term?"

Claudia untied the knot at the back of her neck, slipped out of the apron. "Things aren't going well at home. I've decided to get out of my mom's way."

Hope pretended shock that Claudia would open up so quickly to a stranger. But she knew why: because Hope kept demonic voices whispering in Claudia's ear, hammering at her sanity, telling her what a "safe" person she was. Hope put on her most concerned face. "That might be for the best. You don't want to make a bad situation worse." Such wisdom. She knew the girl was confused.

She would keep working on Claudia. Encourage her to do exactly the wrong thing.

If she couldn't find Patch, she'd torment his friends.

Having purpose in life felt good.

28

PATCH WATCHED THE smoke rise. He had to try something. What if Ned did something reckless, like try to get inside?

Patch stepped into the street, and the green lights on his ankle turned red. He yanked his foot back into the safe zone. Then he turned, raced back into the house past Ma Stone, and dialed 911.

Several minutes later he watched the fire truck roll by as if stuck behind a herd of elephants.

Patch screamed at the driver. "Down there! Go! Go!"

The man waved.

Why so slow?

Patch knew. Because Ned's burning house was God's will.

He heard the shouting, saw flames stroke the sky.

Ma Stone leaned on the doorframe watching him. "Why do you care so much? It's God's will—whatever happens."

Patch looked at her in anguish. "I should be there for him."

She gazed at him a moment, then left, and a minute later he heard her on the phone. She returned. "Go ahead."

What had she done? He took a step into the street. Red light.

Another step. No alarms, no jolting electricity. She must have turned off the sensor. He ran, wondering if he should escape while he had the chance. He was free. No walls, no borders. But he couldn't abandon his new little friend. Not after what he'd been through.

When he neared Ned's house, Patch smelled burning wood, melting plastic, and something worse. The flames roared like a hungry beast. The firemen were there, taking their time hooking hoses to the hydrant. They weren't firefighters. They were fire watchers. They finally began halfheartedly spraying water.

"Hurry!" Patch screamed.

THE SHINING ONE froze, careful to stay perfectly still. He feared that the slightest movement might incite the flames further. Given the right conditions he could cause a windstorm to flare with the fury of a tornado.

Looking around, he felt trapped. Alone. How he wished he could grab a nearby cloud and squeeze out buckets of rain. Soak the swirling, grasping fire below. Do something to stop the destruction.

He'd seen the little boy, Ned, run inside. The child wasn't thinking clearly. That was obvious. He'd slammed the door behind him. How the Shining One wanted to reach through time and space and tear the child from danger. All he needed was a single sign of approval from his Commander.

It didn't come.

For now he could only watch the crawling moments unfold. He shared Patch's frustration. Why wouldn't these people move? How dare they talk about God's will without making a single step to serve as hands and feet for the Father.

Deep breath in, deep breath out.

Love them. Be patient with them.

Just as Jesus would.

Patch had to find Ned. He screamed the boy's name over and over, circling the house. Neighbors watched the fire, wringing their hands. To one side, he saw Ned's parents. Although they were surely professing with their mouths that the fire was God's will, Patch could see the anguish in their eyes, the words not spoken.

No one else moved. Patch was again trapped in the zone where only he seemed capable of action. Everyone else stared stupidly. Forget them. He'd do what he was supposed to do.

Patch dropped to his knees, head down. As someone shouted behind him, he scrambled to the front door. At least he could try to find the boy.

He had no idea where the fire began and ended, but the front door was still cool when he checked with the back of his hand. With a scream, Patch cranked the knob. Then he was inside. Barely a step away he saw the boy, sobbing, flat on his face. Patch skittered forward, head low, and grabbed the terrified child.

Ned nestled into him, his toy monkey over his arm. Both were smoky but safe.

As Patch ran from the house the heat seemed to explode. Windows shattered, glass flew.

Nobody could get in now. Anyone left inside would not have survived. The house was lost to spitting, coiling flames.

Patch carried Ned to his parents. The boy's mother dropped to her knees as Patch placed the child in her arms. She didn't speak; she only held him.

"Thank you." Ned's father's voice caught. "We couldn't stop him. He went back for Gilla."

"The stuffed animal his sister gave him," his mother said. "We thought it was God's will to give him up." She stroked Ned's hair, then burst into tears.

"God's will is not for little girls and boys to die needlessly!" Patch blurted. "It's your job to do everything you can to protect your kids. You're the parents, aren't you?"

They stared at him, and the man spoke. "We did all we were allowed."

Even after what happened they still didn't seem to get it. What was wrong with these people? Patch shook his head and stomped away.

Get out of this town, he thought. *Run!*

It was his only hope. Escape before they reactivated the ankle alarm.

D*ÉJÀ VU.*

Erin and Molly perched on their uncomfortable school chairs waiting for McCry's decree. If Erin's mom found out, she'd be grounded for a decade. Things were tense enough already at home.

Molly looked nervous too.

"You two are slow learners." McCry snatched the computer mouse.

Molly grabbed it back. "I take offense to that. Shouldn't I be able to research my beliefs online? Especially if there's no one I can ask in person?"

Erin cringed. When would Molly learn to shut up?

McCry ranted about how much trouble she could make for them. After seeing the posters, Erin believed her. Totally. This wasn't the time for confrontation, but that wasn't stopping Molly.

"What about students' rights?" Molly asked.

"The only speech that's free," McCry said, "is speech that promotes the common good. But my goal today is not to harass you. I know how you can help everybody."

"Not if you're involved," Molly said.

"All I have to do is let your parents know, and you'll be more than banned from the library. You'll be kicked out of school. Not to mention what could happen to your families. But it doesn't have to be this way. We can work together."

"After you put up those posters?" Erin jumped into the conversation. "They're designed to make everyone hate us."

"Brilliant, aren't they?" McCry looked around the room. A crowd was gathering, whispering, pointing at the girls. Erin felt trapped. Maybe Molly was right. Compromise was impossible.

"What can we do to stop this?" Molly said. Erin thought the girl had turned pale.

McCry turned to Erin. "I assume you've told your friend here about Jenny."

Erin lowered her eyes. Of course she had. She had also sworn Molly to secrecy.

"I'm having a member of my staff videotape the pathetic little thing. Her brother should know she's alive." McCry's teeth glistened. "That's your punishment, Erin. You'll understand why soon."

She turned to Molly and snagged her collar. "Have you seen the posters yourself?" She pinned Molly in her seat.

The girl refused to answer, only glared into McCry's face.

"Of course we've seen them," Erin said. She reached for Molly's hand, craving solidarity. McCry pushed her away.

"We're not afraid." Molly glared at the woman.

Speak for yourself, Erin thought.

"God is on our side." Molly looked at Erin. "Never forget that." She pointed to McCry's silver head. "Please pray for her too."

McCry cleared her throat. "You do and I'll arrest you."

As Erin watched, she dragged Molly away, arms pulled up behind her back. Erin thought of chasing after them. But what good would it do?

She'd only get into deeper trouble.

Erin saw students staring at her. Some faces she knew, acquaintances she'd passed in the hall. All seemed angry. She left before they could decide what to do to her.

H E'D SPENT SEVERAL hours walking around, but now it was decision time. Go back, turn himself in, or run?

Did God want him to go?

He stood in the street before the Stones' house, a few steps from the front lawn.

Sirens whirred, lights flashed, and a Sticklerville police car rolled up.

"What are you doing out here?"

It was the tall cop, the one he had met his first day in town. Next to him sat the heavier one.

"Heading back home," Patch said. After all, he had permission.

"They're not too pleased with you." The man scribbled on a report form. "Pa Stone told us to detain you." His yellow teeth shone. "Scare you a little."

Had the Stones given up on him? "Can I grab my stuff? At least say good-bye?"

"After your verbal assault on those poor people whose house burned down?" He snorted. "Just get in."

Patch slipped onto the hard seat.

"You're bucking against God's will and you need someone to yank back on your reins." The officer's face flushed.

What did that mean? "Where are you taking me?"

"To spend a couple nights in jail."

THE SHINING ONE had seen this before. Many times. The faithful were tossed into a box and hidden from the eyes of others. If they only realized that their seclusion served a purpose. And that they weren't forgotten.

Their faithful songs in the night sounded like choirs in the heavenlies.

God saw them and loved them, even in the darkest places and saddest times. The Shining One hoped that Patch would hold onto his faith.

Such courage, such faith, gave mighty angels a reason to cheer.

THE JAIL STANK of roses, of all things. Someone had plugged in an air freshener.

Not pleasant.

The two officers muttered together, looking at Patch every once in a while. The taller one seemed upset.

"It's their right," was all Patch heard. The door to the police station swung open. Patch smiled at the small figure who stepped through. His parents came behind him.

"Patch." Ned coughed and his voice sounded weak.

"How are you doing?" The boy's face looked peaked.

"You were right," the boy's mom said. "We must do whatever we can to protect our children. It's our responsibility." She teared up. "I'm so glad you opened that front door." She couldn't say anything more.

"Maybe she'd still be here if we hadn't been so afraid," the father said. Patch thought about the little girl in the wagon. About the accident.

"God's will is God's will," the taller officer said. He'd moved closer to the cell.

"Our daughter died because we watched and waited. And didn't get the help we could have quickly enough." The woman held Ned's shoulders. Patch saw that her eyes were red.

"You folks are going to have to leave." The officer took another step toward the family.

"Patch, thank you. For trying. For rescuing Ned." The boy's dad stuck his hand through the bars. Patch shook it.

"If there's ever anything we can do—" the woman whispered; she gave a defiant look at the policeman as they turned to go—"Ask us."

Soon after, the Stones arrived. Despite all the trouble he'd had with them, Patch had never felt so glad to see anyone in his life. They could get him out of here.

"I'm sorry," Patch said.

Ma Stone sauntered to the cell and squeezed a thick arm through the bars, taking Patch's hand.

Pa Stone was angry. He said, "How could you make a scene after that poor family lost their home? And then abuse our trust by running away. What kind of kid are you? That's one of the cruelest things I've ever heard of." He nodded at his wife. "And I don't know what's gotten into her. I think you're hopeless. She wants to give you another chance."

The taller cop said, "Might not make a difference pretty soon." He waved a fax at the couple. "Seems our boy is quite a writer. His WPA essay was one of the state champions. Picked by the governor."

"Congratulations, Patch," the woman said. "I told you it was good."

"Oh, it's quite an honor," the officer said, clearly condescending. "All the state essays get sent on right to WPA headquarters to pick a winner. Whoever that is gets a free trip to California. My son entered and didn't even get an honorable mention."

A trip back to where he'd started from? Maybe these people were right about the will of God. There wasn't much you could do to avoid it.

"Not sure I'd want the trip," Patch said.

"As if you'd have a choice." The man pointed to the fine print. "Winner's gotta collect the prize money in person. Either he heads out there or they send somebody to get him."

Of course. Patch had a feeling what would happen when his essay got to WPA headquarters. He should never have entered.

"Well, that's no matter right now," Ma Stone said. "I still want him with us."

The man shrugged. "Fine. But your leash will be shorter than ever. One step beyond your limits and you'll be right back here."

The threat of two days under lock and key disappeared. Patch watched the cell door swing wide. He wished he'd left town after all. Now he was stuck. Back under house arrest.

29

LEON STOOD ON the edge of the sidewalk. For some reason he didn't seem willing to step on the Stones' lawn. Probably because of the few hours Patch had spent behind bars. Couldn't blame him. Still, Patch appreciated him being brave enough to show up at all.

"It's not so bad here." Leon leaned from side to side like it was impossible for him to stand still. "Just go with the flow."

Maybe the guy was right. Patch had had the chance to run but decided to head back to the Stones. To try to work things out. He scratched at the itchy ankle clamp. "So Denny couldn't make it?"

"Said it wasn't God's will that he hang out with you." Leon looked down. "Gotta run."

What could Patch do? He waved as his friend left.

It might be God's will for things to keep on keepin' on. Nothing different in his routine. Besides, if he'd tried to run he'd be in worse trouble than ever.

Patch pulled at the plastic grasping his leg. Trapped. Alone. Thankfully, the Stones were still civil to him and he had plenty of food.

What more could he want?

Another day, another chance to stare at Marty's face. Granger couldn't get rid of him. Now that the guy understood the power of the demon ring, he wanted to stick close.

"Can I use it?" he said. "C'mon, when can I borrow it?"

"When you're ready. It's not a toy." Despite the constant, annoying questions, given Marty's military training, Granger didn't mind having him around. Maybe he could help protect Hope from Barry. He had to find her. She hadn't been at school the past two days. And Granger was worried.

Finally he asked the ring to help and immediately felt led to try the mall. "Come on, Marty."

They had been there less than a minute when she appeared, looking incredible as always.

Granger dove in. "You know that guy, Barry?"

She nodded. "Nice guy. Kind of cute."

"This may sound strange, but I think he's a demon."

"What in the world are you talking about? Demons aren't real." She snuggled into his arm.

Granger told her how he had worked a deal with a devil named Trevor and gotten his ring. "With it I can read minds. And more."

Marty nodded, obviously in awe of Hope. Who wouldn't be? The girl was out-of-this-world beautiful.

At the moment, though, she looked doubtful.

"All you have to do is look through the center of the ring," Granger said. "You'll see what's really there—including a demon."

Hope looked shocked. "Sounds like quite a tool."

"Here's how it works." Granger held the ring toward Hope's face. She jumped back. "Don't worry. I'll hold on to it." She still seemed jittery. "I'll test it on Marty so you can see there's no problem." Granger aimed his mini-window. "Any demons?"

Marty grinned and waved.

"I don't see anything," Granger said.

Hope smiled and held out her hand. "Can I see it?"

What could he do? She wanted it, so he handed it over. "It definitely works. I've seen it."

After examining the ring, she clamped it tightly in her palm. "Okay, guess it's not working now."

"Yeah, it is. Just means Marty's not a demon." Granger was a little offended. He wanted to protect Hope, keep her from danger. And she was acting like he was trying to put something over on her. Why was she acting so weird? Granger peeled her fingers back and plucked out his ring.

"Let's try aiming it at someone else," Hope said.

"Why not at her?" Marty stuck out a long finger in Hope's direction.

The guy could be so rude.

"She looks scary."

Granger was about ready to punch his friend. "Don't push it, bozo."

Marty's mind seemed to get his mistake. "No, I don't mean Hope. I'm talking about the cell phone saleslady."

Marty was such a social idiot sometimes. He needed to take lessons from Granger.

"As we've already demonstrated," Granger said, "if someone's a demon I find out. Humans aren't demons, so nothing shows up when I ask." He held the ring toward Hope as he spoke.

For some reason Hope crossed her arms over her face. She was so cute sometimes.

"What's wrong, Hope?" Granger slipped the ring into his pocket.

"That thing annoys me. Keep it away."

"Barry bugs me," Granger said. He looked to Marty for support. "He's not of this world, right?"

"You're sure?" Hope asked.

"We're sure." Marty touched his eyelids. "Saw it myself."

Hope brightened. "You guys say it's true, I believe it."

30

PRIVACY WASN'T ALLOWED at Nancy's house. And certainly no locked doors. Her mom didn't trust her.

At least her door was shut. And for the first time since deciding to check on the Bible, she felt it would be safe. She and her mom had just had another argument, and she was sure her mom had no desire to talk to her for the rest of the evening.

Should I be doing this? God, please give me some kind of sign.

Maybe if she bugged him enough, he'd answer. Nancy didn't feel very hopeful though.

She opened the bottom dresser drawer stuffed with sweaters unworn for years. She hurried, feeling under everything until she found a square lump wrapped in tissue. She pulled it out but dared not open it until she made sure one more time that no one would walk in on her.

Getting up, she yanked the door open. She was surprised to find her mom standing there, looking guilty. Or maybe just suspicious.

"After our . . . talk, I wanted to make sure you're okay."

Why would she suddenly care? Nancy looked her in the eye. "I'm fine."

Her mother looked past her. "What's that on the floor?"

"Dad's birthday present," Nancy said.

"Let me see!" She lunged toward the bulky package. "What if I happen to get him the same thing?"

"That's not going to happen," Nancy snapped. "You'll both enjoy it. I don't want to ruin the surprise."

"How about some wrapping paper?"

"Okay, but nothing feminine. No ladybugs or pink bows."

When her mother left Nancy removed the Bible from the tissue paper and jammed it as far as she could under her mattress.

Now what could she use as a gift for her dad? She scanned her closet and yanked down a shoebox.

"This okay?" her mom said, entering without knocking.

TWO DAYS PASSED before she was yanked out of class. Molly was surprised . . . and not surprised. It was exactly the way McCry liked to work. She let you think you were okay—and then *zap!* Gotcha.

Molly lay stretched out on the table. She'd been here before. With Erin. Drugs, needles. Painful prodding. When would she learn to shut her mouth?

McCry checked the arm and leg restraints. "I want you to tell me where Patrick Johnson is." She pinched Molly's cheek and twisted.

Ouch. That would leave a bruise. "Be happy to." Molly shut her eyes. "If you ask nice."

"I'm not able to." McCry lifted one of Molly's eyelids, not gently. "This isn't nap time."

"I don't know. Have no idea." Molly felt a headache building. "Can't you leave him alone? All of us?" Her frustration seethed. This crazy woman wouldn't let up.

"Christ-Kids have no rights." McCry leaned over her, a stinky cherry smell oozing from her mouth. "We'll go ahead and give you the shot. See if your memory improves."

"And then you'll send me home?" Maybe McCry would agree.

"Perhaps. But it'll be back to school with you. No skipping." She patted Molly's hand. "If you won't help me, I'm sure your friends will be able to influence you."

After those posters, no one would give her a moment's peace.

Molly watched the lab assistant jab her vein, push the plunger. The icy liquid invaded her body and she squeezed back tears. In the back of her mind she heard McCry asking questions. And she answered.

She had no choice.

31

WHERE WAS MOLLY today? Erin hadn't seen her anywhere at school. She hoped she was okay. But she had another puzzle to work through in her mind. She ran through every possible alternative. Could she protect Jenny without McCry turning her in?

Before she had an answer, McCry's assistant showed up at the front door. Barry, in the flesh.

He handed her a card meant to impress. She had to admit the guy was kind of cute, but something about his smile made her skin crawl. She could only imagine what was behind the mask.

He looked older, cooler. Had worked on his style issues. Like he'd had a personal shopper or something. But of course she recognized him. Even with an upgraded costume he was still the creep who'd trailed her at Demon's Bluff. Erin wondered where his weird little girlfriend was lurking.

Any friend of Trevor's was an enemy of hers. She'd try to get along and hope he'd get out of here quickly.

"Where's the girl?" His breath smelled of curdled milk.

Jenny bounced into the room wearing her watermelon dress.

"This guy wants to talk to you," Erin said, not hiding her lack of enthusiasm.

"I want to shoot some video of you."

Jenny smiled. "Patch used to take movies of me too." She looked down. "Mom and Dad loved them."

"Would you like to make a movie?" Barry said.

"'Bout what?"

"You," Barry said. "The cutest little thing I've ever seen."

He set up lights and a microphone. "I'm going to get some closeup shots of your face. Your profile."

Jenny smiled and waved wildly at the camera.

"You're going to be famous," Barry said, and Erin thought he flicked his tongue like a snake.

Thirty minutes later Barry hit the Rewind button and checked the playback.

Erin just wanted him out of the house.

"That was fun," Jenny said.

Barry got down on his hands and knees, pretending to care. "Want to make another movie with me sometime?"

Erin wanted to gag. This was the last thing Jenny needed right now. "It's lunchtime. We've got to go." She struggled to keep her voice upbeat.

"Wish I could join you," Barry said, "but I gotta get back to the office."

"Of course you do. Otherwise McCry would have to do her dirty work herself."

Barry sneered, then looked at Jenny. "Your friend's right. I need to go because I want to get your movie online by the end of the day. It's a real-life thriller about a little girl named Jenny who's close kin to an honest-to-goodness fugitive."

Jenny clapped. She didn't understand.

"What are you talking about?" Erin said.

"Jenny is going to help bring back the fugitive. We want this movie to be enticing. You don't know that word, do you, Jenny?"

The child shook her head.

Barry turned to Erin. "You won't have a moment's peace once this hits the Web. We're calling it 'Captured in the Suburbs.' Imagine when he sees it."

"But we're not holding her against her will," Erin said.

"Going to be tough to prove that after people see this. My movie, my special effects, my reality."

MOLLY OPENED HER eyes. McCry's red face loomed like a storm cloud. What had she said? The woman looked mad enough to spit.

"You can't keep this up," McCry said. "All this lying."

"I only tell the truth."

McCry spat on the floor. "This machine helps us convince liars to change their mind."

An assistant rolled up a box—metal with twisted wires of all colors. Molly felt fear grab her spine. The woman used alligator clips to connect metal conductors to Molly's earlobes, eyebrows, and all sorts of sensitive places on her face.

"Electricity."

Molly felt a buzzing on her face, like tiny ants dancing.

"We like our confessions to be unforced, but sometimes we make exceptions."

"What do you want me to tell you?" Molly was tired. She'd rather face her classmates. Anything but this.

McCry nodded. Another zap, a fizzy feeling. Molly opened her mouth to scream, but nothing came out.

"Deny your God." The electrical flow stopped. "That's all you have to do to stop this."

"No. Never." Molly didn't feel strong, though. How much more could she take? Terror crowded out clear thinking.

"You can shorten your torment," McCry said. "Just deny him. Your so-called savior."

"Stop." Molly yelped at another jolt. "I have to tell you something."

McCry leaned in. "We're recording. Go ahead."

"Jesus loves you." Molly smiled. "Get that and you might be able to shorten *your* torment."

McCry stood tall, face red. Molly's prayers never stopped.

32

FIRST SCHOOL, THEN another long shift. She'd barely said hi to Erin, and Nancy avoided her in the hallway. Molly had returned, looking awful, like she'd been in a fight, but she seemed afraid to stop and talk. Claudia had her own problems, so she let her hurry by.

Claudia quickly tired of the coffee stench, and she hated smiling at everybody, pretending she cared.

That morning she'd turned in her essay about finding faith. She'd written it for her mom. She didn't care if she won. Someday maybe her mom would read it and understand what Christianity was. And how much it cost. Literally and spiritually.

For now, though, she was stuck trying to scrounge a few lousy dollars. At least she had a new friend. Hope always seemed to be there, and she always talked sense. After much discussion Hope had convinced Claudia of the best thing she could do to really free her mom.

Leave town.

Claudia wasn't sure. She had an old car, but not much money saved up. "Where would I go?"

"Why worry?" Hope gestured past the glass windows. "Your destiny rests beyond yourself. Past this place."

Claudia liked that. And she had to get away from people who saw her in a negative light.

"I do have a friend . . ." she said.

Hope smiled. "Ooh, a special guy?"

"Not like that." Claudia couldn't explain that it wasn't romantic with Patch. She longed for his grasp of spiritual things.

Hope talked like she'd miss Claudia. "You're not going to tell your mom you're going, are you?" Sweet of her to be worried.

"I've already caused enough problems."

Hope patted Claudia's hand. "You're actually giving her a gift."

WHO CARED? HER face was bruised. She hadn't bothered trying to cover the marks with makeup. Let them see.

Her parents had picked her up last night and driven her home without a word. Not a single question about what she'd gone through. They were angry that she was "pushing limits" again. That she wouldn't give up her beliefs. They called her crazy and worse.

After what McCry did to her, they still made her go to school the next day. "You'll be arrested if you don't."

Molly had heard McCry threatening her parents: "Make sure she's there. She'll be an example to others."

In the hallways kids stared, spat, tried to trip her. Former friends pointed to her face and made crude comments. But God had given her the strength to handle the WPA "examination" room. And he'd be here for her too.

"Jesus loves *you*, this I know." Molly sang quietly to herself. She stood alone, but no way would she back down. She would say what needed to be said, even if former friends backed away. The truth stung. She should know. But she wouldn't hide. If McCry wanted to watch, fine. She would keep telling people about Jesus. He saved them from sin. Why couldn't they see that?

Over the past six weeks her GPA had tumbled. But so what? She'd discovered something far more important. The online Bible studies, the blogs.

Molly's online name was God'sGirl. Patch Meister wrote to her regularly, although she'd quickly determined he wasn't her old friend. Still, he was nice.

But where was the real Patch?

She sat in class, trying to stay quiet, unnoticed. But then her history teacher started babbling about Christians. Called them traitors, haters. It reminded Molly of the day Patch had stood and taken the torment while others watched. While she stared.

Now she slowly stood. She had to. "I used to think the same way you do, but now I know that true Christians show love to one another. Not hate."

"You will be seated immediately."

"Yeah, shut up!" Marty yelled, clenching his hands into knots.

"No. Jesus is God's Son. He died for our sins. He was the perfect sacrifice."

"Bring back the lions!" Marty shouted, and others joined the chant.

Molly's teacher pumped his fist.

"Jesus, forgive them," Molly said, in that instant understanding how Patch must have felt—alone in a crowd, believing a truth that everyone else despised.

God's peace surrounded her and a tear fell. "I love you, Jesus."

The roaring increased. "Lions! Lions! Lions!"

God was speaking to her. *Stand firm. Don't waver.*

She would—no matter what.

PATCH CALLED ERIN. Ma Stone was taking her afternoon nap and Pa Stone had headed out for a walk. Patch's excitement grew as he punched Dial. He loved talking with her, hearing her voice. Would he ever have the opportunity—and the guts—to give her that ring?

When she answered he said, "Can you talk?" He wished he could see her face.

"It's getting worse." Erin told Patch what McCry had done. She'd outed the known Christians. "Molly, Claudia, and me. The whole school knows."

Patch heard a catch in her voice. "What's wrong?"

"They hate us. They've been shouting us down, throwing food, trashing our lockers."

The meanness angered Patch. He wished he could be there, helping somehow. But what could he do? He was just one guy.

"What about that treasure?" Patch had thought of little else. "The thing I left behind?"

"I have to get it to you." A click, then silence.

"What was that?"

"I think Mom might have been listening."

From Patch's perspective he might as well be talking directly to McCry. Yeah, that would work. Having a sit-down with a psycho.

"What about you?" Patch was worried about his friend. "You okay?"

"So far I've survived." Patch wondered how tough she'd really had it.

"I miss you, Erin."

"So do we. Terry and me."

"I have to hang up." Patch didn't want to, but Ma Stone's snoring didn't sound quite so loud as before. He didn't want her catching him with his phone.

"'Bye," Erin said. She didn't say another word.

Patch waited for the click and hung up too.

33

McCry scanned the contest entries. Most writers used false names.

But some poured out personal information, even their addresses and phone numbers. If McCry had asked for bank account numbers, she would've been rich.

She'd had her people send all the local essays directly to her. The whole gang was here: Erin, Molly, Claudia. All well written, all completely incoherent. Each babbled about the reality of a supreme being. McCry wasn't buying it. Never would.

It had almost been too much to hope that Patrick Johnson had entered an essay, but unbelievably, there it was in the state winners' pile. Even an address. Someone must have forced him, hoping for the prize. He wasn't foolish enough to do this on his own. They'd have been better off just turning him in, but maybe they didn't know. Or maybe they believed this contest was legit.

Who cares?

She'd found him.

McCry scanned his story. She was surprised at how well it was written. Nonsense, of course. Who was he, trying to teach her? She was an adult.

One who knew exactly where he lived.

THE ANGEL NAMED the Shining One smiled, delighted to have been assigned to work with the Radiant One again.

"Patrick should not have sent that entry," the latter said. "But he felt he had no choice, and God will somehow use this for his purposes."

"Always," the Shining One said.

CLAUDIA TRUDGED TO her locker. She was exhausted from working a late shift at the coffee shop the night before. She just wanted to mind her own business, shuffle to class.

There were lots of new posters on the walls, slapped on bulletin boards, but she was too tired to check them out. Until she got to her locker.

Her face. Perky, smiling, on a color poster.

Someone had scribbled a mustache over her lip, darkened her brows. She looked demonic. Worse, kids had spray-painted upside down crosses all over. "Keep away. X-girl lives here."

What? Then she got it. X meant "cross."

She noticed clumps of students eyeing her. And they looked angry.

She was marked. Afraid.

How long could she stay?

34

GRANGER FLIPPED THE ring in the air, watched it spin. He'd used it to see Barry's true self. He'd even used it to check out Marty. But he'd been toying with a new idea.

Why not look at himself in a mirror?

"Hey, ring," Granger said. He no longer felt funny talking to the thing. He'd learned that he had to make demands to get what he wanted. "Show me the real me."

He wasn't afraid—not in the least. He knew he'd see warmth, kindness, perfection. No doubt.

Granger locked the bathroom door and held the ring between his thumb and forefinger. It warmed.

He looked through it into the mirror.

An instant later the ring was bouncing on the tile floor.

Granger was sickened. That face, that thing, couldn't be his true self. No way did he have those horrible eyes and sagging folds of skin. The ring had tricked him.

He grabbed the ring and started to stuff it into his pocket. But no. He had to look one more time, to make sure the real Granger was there.

Slowly he forced himself to peer through it again.

The thing was still there. Skin falling in. Neck layered, drowning in oozing tissue, eyes slanted almost to his jaw. His heart flamed red, pounding slowly. Something rose from his chest, a buzzing swarm of misting insects. A sharp putrid scent reached him.

Death.

His soul ached.

He didn't get it. He was such a nice guy. Had once even rescued a damsel in distress. He was pretty decent overall, wasn't he? Wasn't that all that mattered?

She'd known it would happen. Since her stand in the classroom yesterday, she'd been expecting retaliation. Now, twenty-four hours later, hard hands again dragged Molly from her history room, pulling her from the glares of her classmates.

First Patch, now her. How many other Christ-Kids faced such abuse?

Molly's parents would never understand. They'd want to get rid of the problem. Send her to New Peace Clinic.

But it hadn't worked last time. And it wouldn't work now. Molly loved God, and she would do whatever he wanted her to.

The student guards shoved her down the hall to the principal's office; Marty, her old friend, pushed the hardest.

"Move it, Skinny Legs," he said.

Within a few minutes her mother and father arrived, wearing the same expressions as the previous time she'd stood up for what she believed.

"We can't let this happen again," her father said.

"I've never stopped being your daughter," Molly said. "Never stopped trying to tell you how much Jesus loves you, but you—"

"That's enough." Her mother looked around nervously.

The principal took his cue. "Your parents have a few options. One is New Peace Clinic again, perhaps more aggressive treatment this time."

Her father seemed eager, but her mother grimaced. "She was so strange when she got home last time."

"Then you might consider Straight Arrow."

That was where Nancy had gone, where her parents tried to get her back on track. Yeah, Nancy. A picture of real mental equilibrium.

Molly had heard it was a horrible and controlling place, where everything was decided for you. She would suffocate. She begged for New Peace. At least she'd have solitude, time to think and pray. Straight Arrow meant being crammed in with five other girls in a small cabin.

The principal handed her a Straight Arrow brochure. Creepy kids populated the cover. Arms around each other, smiling perversely. Way too happy.

"Straight Arrow it is," her mother said.

"Good choice," the principal said. "The director, Miss Grady, has unique methods of dealing with the disobedient. And Molly will be miles from anyone who might negatively influence her."

Molly had to say it, not knowing when she'd get another chance. "I love you, Mom and Dad. So does Jesus."

The principal smiled condescendingly. "He's a myth, and you've known that all your life."

"Jesus is real. I've seen his power."

"Show me." Her father's voice was raw. "Let me see him. Now."

Molly looked down and shook her head. It was over.

AFTER LEADING THE class against Molly, Marty was stoked. He was ready for more action. For something more concrete. Something that would show McCry he meant business.

Going to the lunch room, he singled out a few friends, whispered in their ears, and started pointing. Then he stood back and watched.

The whispers continued. More people. More pointing, glaring. Grabbing at the posters that lined every wall.

Then the chanting started. "Christians out of school. Christians out of school."

It was picked up by more and more kids. They surged from classes, roaring. "Christians out! Christians out!" Louder and louder.

Perfect.

Marty found Erin cowering in her math class. He pointed and she was quickly grabbed and pulled out. He got more help and went for Claudia, plus a few other kids who looked suspicious to him.

Who cared if he was wrong?

They dragged the kids outside. Erin went along, no fighting, no screaming. Claudia wasn't as calm. Marty would have to watch her.

The mob kept growing. "Two—four—six—eight. Get 'em out 'fore it's too late!" Over and over.

Marty felt a surge of strength. He fed off the confusion.

He looked around. At the edges of the crowd stood the principal and several teachers. They didn't lift a hand or say a word.

Marty wasn't sure who shot the first soda spray. Others grabbed cans from backpacks and shook them hard. Soon a rain of soda showered down upon the captives.

"Leave us alone!" Claudia screamed. She was hugging Erin, who stayed silent.

More spraying fountains of sticky wetness. Soon all the victims were marked, filthy with soda.

"Get out." Marty took the lead. "We don't want you here."

"Bring back the lions!"

Ah, yes. One of Marty's favorite chants. He raised his arms, nodding his head. *Louder, louder*, he thought.

When they ran, Marty started the booing. He smiled as the soaked kids ran through the crowd. People rammed them, tried to trip them.

Let them run, Marty thought. *We know where they live.*

35

Hope stood at Claudia's door, waiting. She'd heard the demonic whispers, knew that something big had happened at school, and had come for details. And more.

Handling this human was easier than Hope would have believed. She felt like a puppet master, forcing Claudia to move. The hardest task was keeping the laughter from spilling out.

"And they yanked us out of class. Soaked us." Claudia had shared every detail, and Hope wished she could have been there.

Of course she'd acted all sympathetic.

"Poor thing," she said. "You definitely need to get away. For your own safety. And to give your mom a new chance."

The girl had bought every line. While Claudia's mother was out, Hope helped her pack.

Now Claudia looked up at her, tears bubbling. "I don't know what to say in the note."

Hope scanned the scribbles. Pathetic. *Blah, blah, I love you, blah, blah, I'm only doing this for you. Whatever.* "Really sweet, Claudia. It will touch your mom's heart."

"I don't know. She might take it the wrong way."

"How about if I talk to your mom?" Whatever it took to get Claudia on the road.

"Maybe I should stay and tell her myself," Claudia said.

"You're in no state of mind for that. You're in pain; she's in pain. Let me do it, as your friend."

"Guess I can visit Molly at Straight Arrow." Nancy had called the moment she'd heard the news.

Stupid, Hope thought. Claudia probably wouldn't even be allowed in. "Yes, she needs you. And your mom needs you to leave."

She helped Claudia lug her bags to the car.

"Thanks for being here for me," Claudia said.

So sincere. So stupid.

Hope waved as Claudia drove away. "I'd go to hell for you, my friend," she said, giggling.

Back inside she tore up Claudia's note, helped herself to whatever she wanted from the fridge, and cranked up the TV. She was in the middle of a movie when she heard a thin adult voice.

"Claudia?"

"Nope, it's Hope." She zapped off the television. Showtime. "Claudia ran away, ma'am."

The woman ran down the hall and tore open Claudia's bedroom door, shouting her name and looking into her drawers and closet. Then she checked the bathroom. Finally she returned.

"What happened?" she said. "I need her."

"That's what I told her. But she said she was tired of all your rules and questions."

The haggard woman's tears spattered her makeup. "That . . . ingrate."

"That's what I thought, ma'am, but she wasn't listening to me."

36

AFTER WHAT HAD happened at school yesterday, Erin was scared. Molly had been sent away. And who knew what Claudia was doing? They were being scattered.

She sat at the ice cream parlor watching Jenny eat, certain the girl was no longer safe. After manipulating Jenny, the WPA had what they needed, and past that she didn't matter to them. Once that video was posted online, both their lives were as good as over. Erin would be marked for sure. She would look crazy, like she was forcing the girl to become a Christian. Brainwashing the child.

They'd send her away and throw away the key, she imagined. And Jenny would be sent off somewhere to be "rehabilitated." Placed somewhere far away, where Patch would never be able to find her. Erin didn't want that to happen. But what could she do?

The whole family's reputation was on the line. Erin had to talk to her mother. They needed to hide Jenny quick. Maybe with a relative.

"How was school today?" The voice dripped with sarcasm.

Great. McCry. Erin was tired. She'd barely had time to clean up after the attack. She just wanted to sit alone with Jenny. Relax. Not worry about anything for a few seconds.

She wasted no time. "So, what happens when you-know-who tries to find Jenny?"

McCry smirked. "It doesn't matter. This wasn't our only effort. We've already located him."

Erin was excited and terrified at the same time. But maybe that meant they didn't need Jenny anymore. They could forget the whole fake-video scheme.

"And what about her?" Erin said, nodding at Jenny, who was happily licking her cone.

"She'll go back to the Home."

The Home? "Can't she at least stay with us until he returns?"

"You think the WPA would entrust a child to somebody like you?"

"Where is the Home?"

"Check the phone book."

Erin finally understood. "When does she need to be ready?"

"Now." McCry grabbed Jenny by the shirt and ripped her from the stool. Her ice cream plopped to the floor and the tears came.

"Help!" the girl cried.

Erin could only watch as McCry dragged Jenny out and into a car. But she returned with a pile of hideous brown shirts.

What in the world?

"You will wear these to school every day."

Erin took one and held it up. They were dirt brown and had the word "Liar" written in squiggly letters on the front.

"I don't want anyone to forget your standing in the community."

THE POOR THING," the Shining One said.

Who could understand the torment of angels, having to see such terror every day? Not being allowed to step in, to alter free will.

He and his ancient friend, the Radiant One, would watch over the child. Like every small one, she was special.

Perhaps later they would be allowed to do more.

From the clouds they could see the car leave the city and head for a huge warehouse.

The Home. They knew what went on inside.

Y OU HELPED DRAG Molly away?" Granger didn't sound enthused. The guy was downright sick.

"It was so cool," Marty said. "I know she had to be scared, but she walked head high, nose in the air, mumbling and muttering."

"Maybe she was praying," Granger said.

"Isn't that what I just said?" Marty sounded high on himself. "Praying is like talking to yourself. Looney."

Granger nodded. He'd seen enough to convince any skeptic, but still, he doubted. Not that there was another world. Not that angels and demons existed. But that he himself had any business on that spiritual battleground. He had enough trouble keeping track of his homework, even with the ring.

"So she's expelled?" he asked.

"Oh yeah," Marty said. "Won't be seeing Miss Priss again."

How could Marty be so happy? Once upon a time, he'd had a crush on Molly.

"Looks good for you, eh?"

"Yup," Marty said. "McCry called me herself. I'm on the inside again. Barry or not. Hey, any chance I could use that ring of yours?"

Granger used to think he could play Marty. Now he wasn't sure.

"Nah, sounds like you don't need it."

Marty's handshake hurt. "I'd make it worth your while."

When he was alone again, Granger looked at his ring. He had to be specific. Yeah. He wasn't looking for demons anymore—he just wanted a quick glimpse of the guy inside. Wonder if Marty's soul matched his macho exterior?

That's what he had to ask the ring.

He jumped up, grabbed last year's yearbook, and looked for a picture of Marty. He wondered if the ring would work on photographs too.

Only one way to find out.

Nancy sat with the Bible in her lap, obsessing about Molly being sent to Straight Arrow. Molly and Patch were so bold they made her feel like a coward. It made sense that her face wasn't plastered on a poster. She didn't even qualify as a Christ-Kid. She'd been barely a Christ-Baby when she'd rejected it all for empty love.

Nancy had nothing in common with Molly and Patch, at least in how they talked about Jesus. She knew the Bible was true and that Jesus was real and that prayer worked. But what had she ever done about it? Nothing except betray her friends for a boy who didn't even like her.

Maybe Molly would tell somebody about Nancy's Bible to get a lighter sentence at Straight Arrow. Or to be spiteful. It didn't sound like Molly, but what if they got to her, made her crack? That place could drive anyone insane.

If Molly ratted her out, the WPA would surely come calling.

The last thing she wanted was to be sent back to that crazy place to see Lori and Miss Grady again. She shivered.

But Molly needed help. Someone to make sure she didn't tell what she knew. *Not me*, Nancy thought. She was getting great grades and was back on the scholarship track.

Surely God would not put her in danger again.

But Molly needed a real friend. And a Bible. That was all Molly was looking for, an opportunity to dig deeper.

Nancy had a Bible. She suddenly realized how valuable that volume was. Molly was willing to be shamed to ask for it. And she had been. By someone she thought was her friend.

Oh, God. Is there anything I can do—should do—to help?

And now Molly was gone. Without the book she desperately wanted. What kind of a person would be so mean? Who besides Nancy?

How could she be so selfish?

Straight Arrow, here I come.

Standing up and readying herself, Nancy suddenly screamed. A bone-chilling, ear-piercing shriek. "Those horrible horned creatures are back! Mom, help! Help!"

Nancy put everything she had into her acting. She'd seen the real things, so pretending wasn't hard.

Her mother came running to find bed sheets flung to the floor, bedspread heaped.

"Those stinky, drooling things are back, Mom!" Nancy said, snuffling.

Her mother shook her head. "Miss Grady said this might happen. I didn't think it would so soon."

Nancy screamed again, covering her eyes.

"I'll call her." Her mom ran down the hall.

All was quiet. Nancy wrapped the Bible in her pajamas and began packing, wanting to prove to her mother that she was going voluntarily. And prove to herself that she could follow through. She knew she wasn't a steady person; her emotions ruled her decisions. And she'd flip-flopped before. But she wanted to do the right thing this time. It was tough, though, when she had no one backing her up. When she had to stand alone. But this time she was sure she was doing the right thing.

She wouldn't do this if she didn't believe God wanted her to. But she sure was scared.

If only Granger was around. Standing at her side, ready to rescue her.

Somehow she doubted that would happen again.

37

CLAUDIA HAD BEEN driving all night and she could hardly keep her eyes open. Gallons of caffeine weren't helping. She nearly pulled off the highway when the news report came on: "A newly posted undercover video shows that fugitive teen Patrick Johnson's sister, Jenny, has been held captive by a local student, Erin Morgan. Her parents claim they had no idea, thinking she was just being kind to a stray child.

"Authorities say they have determined that the teen kidnapped the child and has been attempting to brainwash her."

Erin's voice came on. "God is real, Jenny. God is real, Jenny." Again and again. It made Erin sound nuts.

What a crock.

Besides visiting Molly, Claudia would pray for Erin and perhaps try to find her too. At least she was fully awake now.

By now, Claudia's mom already knew she was gone. Hope would have explained everything. What a friend.

I'VE BEEN PRAYING that you'd be healed," Patch told Ma Stone.

Embarrassment showed on her face. "We all have to die sometime, Patch. Someday you'll understand."

"But I want you around a while longer," Patch said.

The woman shifted in her chair. "Doc says the cancer's eating me alive."

No wonder her dresses hung like sacks.

"God could still perform a miracle."

"Maybe," she said sadly. "But not for me."

"I'm stubborn. I'll keep praying."

Pa Stone came in. "They're coming for you, Patrick." The man sounded gleeful. "Guess they don't trust you to fly by yourself."

Patch stared out the front door. What if he punched his way through the screen and ran? Would they shock him? He looked down at the reactivated ankle bracelet. Would the pain knock him out? Only one way to find out. He glanced over his shoulder.

"Don't even think about it, boy. WPA faxed the police station. Guy named Barry will be here by morning to go with you on your flight. Get packing, kid."

Patch's heart raced. Trevor's friend. And with Barry around, Hope was probably close by. He knew how these demons worked—they could change their appearances. But if Patch looked carefully, he would still see the creepy fiends hiding behind the human masks.

One thing was sure. The moment they laid hands on him they'd hustle him to McCry. Or worse.

Patch had no choice. He had to get out of there.

When the man left the house, Patch dared to hope that Ma Stone would help.

"Do you know the release code, ma'am?"

Her lashes fluttered and she shook her head. "Only Pa knows the new one."

Patch would never be free, especially once Barry got there. Was he really accompanying him to California? Not likely.

HOPE WANTED TO bare her claws and scratch the silly woman. Claudia's mother was boring her to death, scuffing her fuzzy blue slippers all over Hope's nerves.

Get over it already, Hope wanted to say. Her daughter had already been gone for hours—all night in fact. And Mom was acting like it was the end of the world. What a weird affection these humans showed for each another. What freaks.

Hope definitely didn't get it.

"You can stay as long as you like," the woman said. "It's going to be lonely around here."

"Thanks, but I'm leaving on a trip tomorrow."

The pathetic woman couldn't know Hope was on call, heading to a small town in Kansas with Barry. Sticklerville. A beautiful place to visit, but Hope wasn't planning on staying long. She and small towns did not mix well.

McCry. The fool. She thought Hope and Barry were going to pick up her prize. She'd learn. They took their orders from elsewhere.

They would be toasted for their achievement.

Hope could hardly wait to slip out of human form and into something more terrible.

ERIN CAME TO school in her brown shirt. "Liar! Liar! Liar!" she heard kids chanting, and felt the spit of several.

Someone shoved her into the lockers. Another slapped books out of her hands.

Was she the only one left?

Where was Molly? Taken for retraining.

Claudia? Nowhere to be seen.

Nancy? Out of sight.

She was it. Alone and scared.

Molly touched her cheek. The slap still burned.

"Lori, you shouldn't have done that," Miss Grady said. "At least not with me standing here." Her laugh crackled like kindling.

Lori set her jaw. "Molly will get along just fine, once she figures out the rules."

"I forgive you," Molly said.

"I don't want your forgiveness." Lori's grin disappeared. "I reject it."

Molly took the only open bunk, one next to a window.

"Lori will get you whatever you need," Miss Grady said.

Great.

"How about some towels, soap?"

"Like I said, ask Lori."

Tears came, but Molly didn't care. The others were watching. She unpacked, shoving her clothes into a rickety dresser.

This was home for now.

"God help me."

38

ERIN BARELY SURVIVED the day. She ran home from school weeping. Her mother handed her a glass of ice water. No sympathy, but Erin didn't expect any. They moved on from her worries, which her mother brushed off, to the topic of Jenny.

"Of course I knew what they were planning, Erin," Mrs. Morgan said. "You think I would allow a child like that in this house unless I was sure that she presented no danger?"

"You've heard of the Home?" Erin said.

Her mom tapped Erin on the head. "Of course. The WPA's orphanage."

"So you had no intention of keeping Jenny here?"

"Are you kidding? You and Terry are more than enough."

"Then why?"

"We needed a new car, Erin. They paid us to keep Patch. You think we'd take care of his little sister for free?"

"How could you do this? Don't you care about anyone?"

"Erin, you haven't cared about this family for quite some time. And once this is over, I'm not sure what we'll do with you. The Home isn't only for children Jenny's age. McCry thinks it might do you some good."

Erin just shook her head in disbelief.

"Your father and I cannot believe what you've been doing behind our backs," her mother said. Her words seemed so carefully chosen, Erin suspected McCry had planted a bug in the room.

"What are you talking about?"

Erin's mom went into the den, where she clicked on a video from OpenEyez.com. The camera's grainy, shaky picture played as Barry spoke of "poor little Jenny" and how she was being "tormented by one Erin Morgan."

Erin wanted to laugh at the low quality, the cheap feel of the production. But now was not the time.

"This is not good for our family."

Erin chewed her tongue. Anything to keep from saying what she felt. *This was your idea. You were in on it.*

"I thought you liked her," Terry said, sounding scared. He had tiptoed into the room. "Why did you hurt her?"

"I love her," Erin began. "Everything you saw was a lie. Somebody played a game with their camera and the computer. I'd never hurt Jenny any more than I'd hurt you."

"That's not what Mommy said."

"Go play," Mrs. Morgan said. "Erin and I have to talk."

Erin winked at Terry and mouthed, "I love you."

He did the same as he left.

Her mother shut the door. "We've tried over and over, Erin."

"I'm not trying to be difficult."

"Yes, you are." Her mom patted the chair across from her desk. Erin sat. "You've been nothing but difficult since you met that boy Patch."

"You and Dad volunteered to put him up at our place." Erin thought about how she hadn't been able to stand the guy when he first showed up. They'd quarreled constantly. Her feelings had changed since then.

"But don't you see how he's poisoned you?" Her mom's eyes looked tired.

"No. He freed me. Helped me see that there's more to this life than school, prom, sports." Erin slipped off the chair, crouching at her mother's feet. "He showed me that Jesus is real. Prayer is real."

"He pulled you out of our hearts."

"I love you, Mom." Should she say what was on her tongue? She felt like she was supposed to. "I love Jesus even more."

Her mother plucked Erin's hands from her knees. "That's the kind of talk that worries me."

Erin returned to her chair. "What do you mean?"

"Terry. You're a bad influence."

Oh no.

"We don't want you around him anymore."

Erin felt the tears collecting. She'd messed everything up. Why couldn't she comply like every other kid in school? "I love Terry."

"Perhaps we should place you in the Home until we figure out what's best for the family."

Family. Erin realized she wasn't considered a part of that group anymore. But she tried anyway. "Please, let me stay."

"McCry offered us priority placement for you at the Home." Her mom sighed. "Quite a privilege, actually. Plus she can keep an eye on you. Something to consider . . ."

Erin could only watch as her mother walked from the room, high heels tapping.

39

THE HOME LOOKED perfect from the outside. Large picture windows. Huge fenced yard. Lots of room to run and play. But the Peaceful One knew the lawns were pristine only because no small feet were permitted to muss them.

The Peaceful One heard Jenny's tears—tiny drops echoing like boulders shoved over a cliff. She cried alone, curled in the corner of a stiff leather couch, as other children walked by. Hers was not the only sad face.

The Peaceful One wished he could comfort the little girl. But for now, he could only watch and pray.

Women milled about wearing white lab coats, heels clicking on tile. Scribbling on clipboards.

It appeared that these children were part of some grand experiment. Those in charge apparently wanted to determine how many children could be cleaned and cared for within a certain period of time. And within a certain budget.

Children were divided by age, herded to various rooms for indoctrination. For training. To be taught the truth as the WPA saw it.

The Home looked like a big comfortable house, but the Peaceful One knew it was all a show. From his view it looked like a maze.

"You better stop," an older child told Jenny.

"But I'm afraid," she said. "I don't know why I'm here."

"It's okay," the girl said, peeking to be sure no one was looking, then giving Jenny a quick hug. "We're all scared."

The Peaceful One smiled. Someone cared.

LAST TIME NANCY had been forced to go to Straight Arrow she'd had a ring, like Granger's. This time it was just her. No spirit voice, no guide. Except God. She wished she could hear him better.

She sure hoped Lori was gone.

No such luck. As she stepped off the bus with her suitcase, she heard her.

"Move it, Molly."

So it had begun already. Molly was lugging a huge load of firewood, her ponytail loose, thick hair in her face.

Lori looked over and saw Nancy. For a moment her face twisted, then she smiled and tripped Molly. Molly tumbled, dropping every last piece of wood. Without a word, she slowly stood and gathered the kindling.

"Clumsy. Hurry!" Lori flashed a thumbs-up and two girls scurried up behind Molly with a large bucket and dumped goo over her head. The sticky stuff covered Molly. A mixture of peanut butter and honey and chocolate syrup.

Lori looked Nancy in the eye. "An old friend taught me how to concoct this mess. To keep my enemies off balance."

Molly sobbed. Nancy reached to help her to her feet. Molly pulled back, then apparently realized who it was. Though her eyes showed her surprise, she made sure not to indicate she knew Nancy. Somehow they both knew it wouldn't be prudent.

"Thanks," Molly whispered. She held her head high, stepping over the wood as Nancy led her to a watering trough for the horses.

Lori stuck a finger in Nancy's shoulder. "I'm in charge here. Molly works for me."

As Molly tried to rinse the gunk from her hair, she turned and spoke with a clear voice. "No. I serve God."

Nancy could not believe her calmness.

"For shame," Miss Grady said, suddenly standing shoulder to shoulder with Lori. "We don't allow that kind of language here. You're cleaning the latrines for the rest of the week."

"Yes ma'am," Molly said. "Happy to do whatever I can to help."

"Really. You're happy?"

"I'm just following God's example."

"You would do well to shut up."

A NICE-LOOKING guy in his early twenties slipped off the stool at the guardhouse at Straight Arrow and sauntered up to Claudia's car window.

"I'm here about the job."

"Kitchen help?" the man said. He eyed her like a connoisseur. "You're too pretty for that kind of work."

Oh, please. "And I'm too smart for that line, especially from a guy wearing a wedding ring."

He opened the gate.

A few minutes later Claudia found the kitchen supervisor and enthusiastically sold the woman on her experience, most recently in the coffee shop. Faster than she could catch her breath, the job was hers.

A WHOLE BORING day crawled by before Barry and Hope got word from slow-as-a-turtle McCry that it was time to fly. They got to the airport pronto. Once there, Barry lapped up the first-class travel. He was ready to relax.

When undercover, they had to settle for the slower modes of travel—like any other human. Not quite as fast as winging himself from one place to another, but not as tiring either. Barry didn't mind a bit. He hit the Steward button, demanding chips and hot salsa.

Hope stared out the window. What was up with her? Sure wasn't paying him as much attention as she used to. That was okay. He wasn't supposed to make friends. Only temporary alliances.

Barry pointed to his laptop, nudging Hope. "Look who wants us." He opened a message from McCry. Barry mimicked her whiny voice. "You are to bring the subject immediately to WPA headquarters so we can manage the publicity."

Hope giggled.

"Your wish is our command," Barry typed.

"She'll be so disappointed," Hope said.

"Not as bright as she looks."

40

GRANGER SLAMMED THE yearbook shut. Wow. He'd seen enough.

The pictures told only half the story. Everybody looked their best. Hair combed, smiling, earnest and hopeful. Lots of pretty girls. Handsome guys.

But when he said, "Let me see the soul inside," the ring showed him something different. He could see them as they were. Get a glimpse of the kind of people they really were behind the poses.

Like his old pal Marty. His eyes looked like waxy dough. His teeth looked like a wild beast's, hungry for prey.

They all looked like that. Behind the happy faces, Granger saw wicked expressions, split tongues, evil hearts. No matter when the picture was taken, he knew he was seeing the person's current spiritual state—just like he'd been shown his own true self.

The ring gave him a snapshot into the soul.

Granger found the short girl with glasses again. Nice timid smile. The ring magnified what hid behind her plain face. She rejoiced, hands raised, smile wide, eyes bright. She gazed heavenward.

That's who she really was. A special person, someone who knew she was loved.

Granger was ashamed he'd made a point of ignoring her.

Then he saw Molly's face. The ring showed the truth. She was beautiful, bright, open, and unafraid. Her eyes were supersized. She was honest—the same inside and out. Yup, that was Molly. The Molly he knew today.

The one Marty had helped drag out of school.

Claudia. Erin. He checked their pictures. The same sunlit souls shone before his eyes. What was it about these Christ-Kids? How could they be joyful when their whole world was crumbling?

What about him? Smug and skinny.

Granger held the ring over his face once more. The horrid figure reappeared. Eyes filled with pus, skin in folds, nose twisted as if sniffing an alley aroma.

That was who he was. Guess he couldn't do much about it. So why even bother worrying about the Christ-Kids? He'd never be one of them, right?

ERIN WASN'T SURE what would happen next. What did God have in mind? School was a nightmare. Jenny had been taken away. Her friends had disappeared.

At least she was home. For now.

Her mother suddenly rushed back into the room. "Look what you've done!" she shouted, shoving Erin to the front window.

On the lawn stood a mob of teens. Many she'd waved to in the halls over the years, others she considered close friends. Only now they didn't look friendly. They carried torches.

"Come out! Come out!"

A rock smashed through the pane, almost hitting Erin.

Her first thought was for Terry. Was he playing in his room? Would the crowd burn their home?

She snuck another look. Marty and Granger launched bottle rockets, tossing them into the clump of kids. Probably trying to rile them. As if they needed more encouragement.

"Come out!" The chant grew louder. Erin looked at her mom, her dad. They had their arms around each other. Her mom shrugged.

"Open up!" a loud, familiar voice. "We need to put Erin some-where secure."

Erin looked through the peephole. It was McCry and her per-sonal escorts.

Her dad swung the door open.

"Maybe now you'll see how your decisions affect all of us," her mother said.

Great, Erin thought. Her mom had taken that last moment to give a speech. Not to say good-bye, not to cry, not to hug her.

Erin felt rough hands leading her out the door. People pelted her with rough words. The escorts held up shields, and rocks bounced off them as they shoved her into their car.

"To the Home," McCry said to her driver.

41

THE PEACEFUL ONE had the gift of focus. So closely did he watch Jenny that the other children disappeared into colorful blurs.

His assigned child ate slowly. She sipped her milk alone amid the lines of children. The room's fluorescent lights glared, yet the atmosphere was still dreary.

Mouths moved as they chewed food, but no words escaped. No giggling, no smiles. The only noise was piped elevator music. Every bite of food on the plate disappeared—or enforcers appeared.

Children should not be forced to sit like soldiers.

The Peaceful One had watched over the ones in the Home for years. During his tenure he learned about God's special children, those whose parents stayed faithful to Jesus even to the point of death. These children had a place to stay and food to eat—but no love.

Unless these kids eventually denied God, they would never leave. Some said the words, hardened their hearts, and turned their backs on this weary life just so they could leave. The Peaceful One had seen it and wept.

When permitted, he encouraged with whispered words of hope. Some listened; some covered their ears.

Jenny scraped the last mouthful off her white plate.

When the meal was over, the children filed into the playroom, a warehouse of sterilized toys, puzzles, computer and video games. No books.

And nothing children could play together.

Apparently the last thing those in charge wanted was friendships.

The Peaceful One praised God at the arrival of a visitor.

"Hey, cutie," Erin said. The angel knew the teen was worried, afraid to be here. But she was being brave. An example for Jenny.

The child looked down at her sneakers with neon laces. She shoved a half-finished puzzle aside and burst into tears. Erin gathered the girl into her arms, and the little one would not let her go.

"Why? How?"

"God wanted me here with you."

"Let her go," an orderly said. He looked like a weight lifter.

Erin held Jenny's hand. "She's my sister."

"Fine. Whatever." He stomped away. Erin looked at Jenny. "Maybe not by blood, but God is our father. That makes us sisters."

The Peaceful One was pleased that Erin stood her ground. But he knew she would pay.

That was how the game was played.

P ATCH STOOD IN the doorway, baggy luggage nestled against his sneakers. It held some clothes, a couple books.

"Can I wait outside?"

It was getting dark. Pa Stone put down the newspaper he'd walked downtown to purchase. "You'll remain where I can watch you until Ms. McCry's crew picks you up."

Patch went to Ma Stone and knelt. "I'm going to keep praying for you."

The man stood. "Get back by the door."

She smiled. "Thanks, Patch."

Patch walked to the door. Now was the moment.

"Good-bye," he said.

"What are you doing?" the man hollered.

Patch pushed the screen door open and stepped out. No pain, no electricity. No screaming sirens. Nothing. Just as he'd suspected, they'd turned them off in preparation for his departure. Couldn't have him setting off buzzers all the way back to California.

Or . . . maybe God had deactivated the ankle chains. Freed him for real the moment he gathered up the courage it took to run.

As he took off, Ma Stone called out, "Keep praying!"

God bless her.

His legs churned as if in a race. Up one street and down the next he ran. No sound of anyone pursuing him. Where could he go?

He found himself outside a trailer. When he looked closer, he recognized the car parked out front. He saw a goofy gorilla toy jammed in the backseat. It couldn't be . . . But God moved in mysterious ways. Apparently he'd sent Patch directly to the place Ned's parents had moved into after the fire.

There was only one way to find out. He knocked on the open door. Inside he could see a few boxes, a pile of toys. The fire must have destroyed almost everything they had.

"What are you doing here?" Ned's mom said, her husband peering from behind her. "Are you all right?" She seemed worried. Obviously they knew he wasn't supposed to be there.

Patch told them he had simply bolted. "But they're coming to drag me away."

The man spoke to his wife. "There's nothing left for us here."

Watching their faces, Patch was afraid to move. Hope squeezed him.

Ned came into the room. The child whooped when he saw Patch, grabbing him around the knees. His mother shushed him—but with a smile on her face.

Ned's father nodded, his decision made. "You saved our boy. We can surely help you now."

They moved quickly after that, throwing their few belongings into the trunk of their car, watching to see if the police were coming. Finally the man said, "Get in the car, Patch. I think we'll take a nice leisurely road trip today."

Patch tore out of the trailer, leaped into the backseat, and slumped to the floor. He slipped an old blanket over his shoulders. Ned reached under to hold his hand.

Patch heard sirens as the car slowly pulled out. Only God could protect them now.

Babbling humans barely registered in Barry's ears. He pushed past a smelly, nervous person claiming to be Pa Stone. The man was scared to the bone.

Barry didn't care. All he wanted was Patch.

Hope slipped into position next to the woman in an old chair. Ma Stone's breath came fast.

"You let him escape?" Barry's voice rose. A roar issued from him and flames seared the wallpaper. The man gawked. *Worthless,* Barry thought.

Hope joined him, leaning her head back and howling.

The woman huddled deeper. These people were idiots, worthless.

Barry growled, shoving Pa Stone to the floor. He had to resist the temptation to destroy this bug. Human fear filled his nostrils. Sweet and powerful. His demon form bulged, threatening to burst from his human costume.

Barry ripped the screen off its hinges and flung it onto the grass. If they didn't locate Patch soon, they'd shed their skins so they could travel faster.

Nancy and Molly worked together mopping the dining room floor.

"I can't believe how you got here," Molly said.

Nancy felt good being the hero for a change. But she was also ashamed. "I was losing—no, I *lost*—my connection to God. I knew it was wrong; I knew I was turning my back on the gang. But I just—"

Lori barged in, her oversized boots filthy with tar, the gunk spattering their clean floor. She looked down. "Oops. They just paved the parking lot. Hurry. I'd hate for you to get in trouble."

"You didn't have to hurt her to get to me," Nancy said.

"Yeah," Molly said, "we all hide hurts. Is that what you're doing?"

"Shut up, Miss Perfect," Lori said.

"Jesus was hurt too."

"Good." Lori spat on the floor. "Maybe he can understand what I'm going through." Her voice wavered.

"He knows what it's like," Molly said. "How you feel."

Lori stomped from the room.

"Hopeless," Nancy said.

Molly surveyed the mess. "So were we."

Claudia shut the kitchen door.

She didn't want Molly and Nancy to know she was there to watch their backs. Not until she'd figured out what to do next.

42

THE CAR ROLLED to a stop. Patch had feared this would happen. A roadblock at the THANKS FOR VISITING sign on the way out of Sticklerville.

Patch recognized the voice of the officer from jail. "Checking for that young fool. Haven't seen him, have you?"

If the officer opened the back door, he could yank Patch from the floorboards.

"What are you talking about?" the man said. "We're taking a little drive. Not much for us to come home to right now."

"You better not be playing games with me. You know what happens if you do."

Patch held his breath.

"Are you threatening us?" Ned's dad sounded weary, his voice full of pain.

"I'm sorry about your loss," the officer said. "But you folks brought it on yourselves."

Under the blanket, Ned squeezed Patch's hand. Patch willed himself not to move.

The officer paused, and Patch wondered if he was looking around the interior of the car, at Ned, at the hastily bagged belongings. "Now don't tell me you folks are trying something stupid, like leaving town. You wouldn't do that, would you? Church folk are supposed to stick close. Once you become part of Sticklerville, you're bound to stay for life. No questions asked."

"Or answered," Ned's father said. "I don't see much life here."

"Where'd you hide him?"

"Why in the world would that boy come to us?" Ned's mom said. "You forced us to run him off when he dared pray for our little girl."

"When he ignored the Sticklerville code," Ned's dad said, "you put him under house arrest."

"You better not leave town."

"Or what?" the woman asked. "What do we have left?"

Another pause, then Patch heard the officer walking away. Perspiration dripped down Patch's back as the car began to move again.

"You were praying, weren't you, Patch?" the woman said.

Patch warily raised his head, then climbed onto the seat. "How did you know?"

"We could tell."

Sticklerville disappeared behind them.

"We'll drive all night if we have to," Ned's dad said.

Patch took Ned's hand and watched the boy fall asleep.

Barry and Hope barreled into the police station.

"Who are you two?" the skinny man behind the desk asked.

"Didn't you hear McCry was sending experts to handle the prisoner transfer?"

The man raised his eyebrows. "Yeah, I heard. But I don't see any professionals around here."

"This won't look good in our report," Hope said, eyes ablaze.

The man snorted. "All we were told to do was turn over the kid." He pretended he was busy.

"So you didn't post a guard on him?" Barry asked.

"Our procedure is no business of yours. Why don't you wait outside until we have Patrick ready for you?"

"He's missing," Barry said. "Or haven't you heard?"

The man looked away. "We, *ahem*, heard something was going on. My partner went to check. I'm sure it's under control by now."

Hope crept toward the desk like a cat sneaking up on dinner. "You're sure of no such thing."

"Look, miss," the officer said mockingly, "if the boy's on the run, we'll find him."

Hope snorted. "You couldn't find your gun with both hands."

"Show some respect," the officer said. Standing, he puffed out his hollow chest.

"You have no idea who we are, do you?" Barry said.

He reached for his hat. "Course I do. Couple of city brats."

Hope roared, struggling with the release latch beneath her hairline. She stripped off her suit and green skin flashed. She kicked off her human covering with a clawed foot, the horns over her eyes flashing like knives.

The officer scrambled into the jail cell and rolled into the corner.

"Think that'll keep you safe from her?" Barry said.

Hope moved toward the man, clicking her jaw, swishing her tail. Her roar shattered two glasses of Coke on the desk.

When another officer rushed in, his partner shouted a warning, but Hope snatched the newcomer's ankle with her tail and lifted him into the air, bashing his heels against the ceiling. Flecks of plaster fell. She tossed the second man into the cell, kicked the door closed, and swallowed the keys, whacking her chest to get the key ring to go down.

With a smirk, Barry tossed Hope her disguise, and she was soon back in her teen princess outfit.

"It's a small town," she said. "We'll find him."

ERIN FELT LIKE Wendy from *Peter Pan*. She was one of the few older children in the Home, and the little ones flocked to her. They were so lonely, looked so scared. Erin's heart broke for them.

Jenny stuck close to her. The orderly had stopped bugging them; he must have realized she made the children more manageable.

"When are we leaving?" Jenny said.

"Soon, I hope. No promises."

Suddenly McCry towered over them.

"More family troubles, Erin?" McCry grabbed Jenny's hand. Her cherry-laced breath assaulted Erin. "I hoped you had matured. To be sent to the Home means they're still babying you."

The woman was delusional. She was the one who'd ripped Erin out of her house.

Erin pushed past her.

"Jenny's not going anywhere," McCry said. "But you, on the other hand . . ." She left the words floating.

Erin was tired of being jerked from one extreme to the other. She wheeled. "On the other hand, what?"

McCry clamped her arm.

"Ow!"

"Keep your voice down," McCry said. "We don't want to upset the kids."

WHAT WAS WRONG with him?

Whenever he was alone and near a mirror, Granger pulled out the ring and saw new details, new reasons to fear. Each time he glanced through the window into his soul, the same pulsing beast stared back. Hungry, wicked, snarling.

How do I get rid of it? Who could he turn to?

Nancy was gone. Molly and Claudia too. And he'd helped scare Erin out of her house.

A chill filled him. He thought of the fire, the rocks, the screaming. Why had he done it? He hadn't thought he was capable of that. But somehow, when Marty showed up and told him the plan, he'd wanted to be a part of it—to feel the power Marty was enjoying these days.

And, he hated to admit, it had been fun.

Granger was scared. He was becoming more sick and twisted. All because of the ring. The image of himself was accurate. He was horrible inside.

And he felt alone. Him and the ring. No way would God listen to him now, especially the way he looked inside.

Unless . . . Nancy was right.

He looked at the ring again. Then, before he could talk himself out of it, he dropped the ring into the toilet and flushed. Good-bye.

Now maybe he could pray again.

God might even listen to him.

43

Y OU SURE ABOUT this?" Ned's father asked, shaking Patch's hand.

"Doesn't look like much of a town," the woman said. Ned stretched and mumbled about needing a bathroom.

"I've got a good friend here," Patch said. Demon's Bluff, now Angel's Point, brought back a pile of memories. He remembered how the sun had been blocked by the horde of demons howling in the clouds. He remembered the scramble as people ran when the attack came. And he pictured his friends, trying to help him, smashed down by the clawing, crushing blows of an army of devils.

"I'll miss you," Ned said. Patch felt the same about the boy. They shared a hug.

He waved as the car pulled away. They'd driven through the night and would have driven him straight to Jarrod's doorstep. But the fewer people who knew, the better. Besides, this little family needed to flee and find a new place to live.

He made it to Jarrod's in half an hour, knowing he couldn't stay long. Wouldn't take much for Hope, Barry, or McCry to figure out where he was.

He was greeted with much love. "Of course, you're welcome,"

Jarrod's mom said, smiling and hugging him. "We thought we'd never see you again."

"I need to talk to Jarrod."

"You're like a brother to him." She handed Patch a glass of goat's milk.

He helped with dinner, keeping an eye on the clock. Finally Jarrod arrived home from school asking if there was anything to eat. Same old Jarrod.

Patch called out, "Too late. I already snarfed it all."

Jarrod crutched his way into the kitchen. "What in the world?"

After an embrace and laughter, they headed for the front porch with a plate of cookies, and Patch told his story—all he'd seen and done since he left. He finished with, "And I've got a couple of demons tracking me."

"Only two?" Jarrod's grin spread to his eyes. "Good thing you came to me."

IT WAS TOUGH for Patch to ask for help. Difficult for him to admit he couldn't figure everything out on his own. The Shining One didn't understand why humans so often let relationships lapse.

They had no idea what awaited them. Last time a mass of heavenly host had been there to help. The situation was different now. Other matters around the globe required a new configuration.

"Think we can handle it?" the Shining One said.

"We have no choice," the Radiant One answered.

He saw the humans bow their heads. Good.

I'M BUSY. OTHERWISE I would." The woman wagged her wooden stirring stick toward the door leading into the dining room, assigning Claudia greeting duty.

"I'm really, really shy," Claudia said. "And I have a cold. You don't want them to get my germs."

The woman blew out a puff of air. Her bangs fluttered. "Wear a sanitary mask. A wonderful opportunity for personal growth awaits you. The Kitchen Queen has spoken."

Claudia had to laugh. Besides having a great sense of humor, the woman was a pretty good cook too.

The face mask fit like a hand over Claudia's mouth and nose and provided a disguise. Plus her hair was pulled back and covered by a cap. Which was good. She still didn't want Molly and Nancy to know she was here. At least not yet. She'd decided she was going to help them get out of here, but she hadn't worked out the details. It wouldn't be easy with high fences all around, not to mention the guardhouse.

Claudia carried in pans of food as the girls gathered, chattering.

"Must be pretty ugly to have to hide behind a mask," someone muttered. The words pierced. Claudia used to be the same way. The old manipulative Claudia would have owned this room. That's why they'd called her the Claw. No mercy.

Let them talk.

Here came Lori.

Something pulled at her ankle and she went flying, mashed potatoes landing like a bomb as the ceramic bowl exploded. Claudia was covered.

The old Claudia would have beat up somebody.

Lori laughed and her groupies gathered like geese. "Clumsy," Lori said. "But maybe she's a good cook."

"Not very good at walking," another said. More laughter.

Molly and Nancy rushed to her, exactly the pair she did not want to see yet—and the ones she missed the most.

"You okay?" Molly said. Her eyes seemed to pierce right through Claudia's disguise. Did Molly recognize her?

Claudia looked down.

"I saw what they did," Nancy said.

They helped Claudia to her feet.

Claudia's tears crept out. "I'm okay," she said slowly, nothing like her confident self.

"We can help," Molly said.

Claudia waved them off. So what if she came across as rude? She had to play it this way for now.

44

P ULLED FROM HER parents' house, torn from the Home. And now here, in McCry's office. Erin felt disoriented. And after hearing McCry's plan she wondered if she was going deaf.

It seemed too easy. Painless. Erin had expected some bizarre torture.

"That's all I have to do?" Erin said. Nothing much, really. And yet, everything.

McCry had planned to have Patch turn traitor and tell the world about the glories of the WPA. Since he wasn't around she needed someone else willing to sell their soul to save their family.

Erin had no choice. McCry was threatening to send Terry to the Home. No way she could allow that.

And it was better than going home to her family. After being yanked from her home and the Home, she knew it wasn't her choice where she lived. She had no power. But after the attack at her house she feared returning. She didn't want Terry or her parents to be hurt. Or Jenny.

"I don't want to hear about Jesus," McCry said. "Or sinners. Or prayer." She paced. "Talk about how smart kids like you have come to see the WPA in a new light and now respect it."

Erin could do that, read a few hokey lines McCry's writing team wrote. She was already a public figure thanks to Barry's stupid video. "Will people listen after Barry ruined my reputation?"

McCry shook her head and spoke slowly, as if to an infant. "People believe what we tell them to believe. We'll leak a story about how the whole kidnapping thing was made up by someone who feared the truth."

"In other words, you'll *tell* the truth?" Erin said. Was McCry even capable of that?

"As long as you participate in our campaign, your family will be safe."

Erin hoped her parents realized she was doing this because she loved them.

And she hoped Terry would learn she'd had no part in hurting Jenny. This was the only way she knew to keep him out of the Home.

Y OU REALLY THINK a police car is a good idea?" Hope checked her lipstick in the rearview mirror. She made Barry crazy sometimes.

"Cut that out!" he shouted, adjusting the glass. "I can't see."

"Why not just will ourselves where we want?"

The girl must have been taking stupid pills. "We're in human form now. Check the mirror again, Hopeless."

Barry finally understood Trevor's desire to work alone. No one bugging you with questions.

"Besides, we can drive as fast as we want. Nobody's going to stop a cop car."

She flashed him a smile. "And if we knew where to go, your plan would be perfect."

"Either Johnson chose a random route, or he headed someplace familiar."

"Well, that narrows it down."

But Hope perked up. A fang showed, as it often did when she was trying to figure something out. "Barry, are you thinking what I'm thinking?"

He looked at her and slowly nodded. "Next stop: Demon's Bluff."

Barry floored it, running red lights with the siren blaring.

"What are we going to do with him?" she said. "Not deliver him to McCry, of course."

"Take him to the council for judgment and torture, not necessarily in that order."

They laughed. As the car heated up from the sulfuric fumes of their breath, Barry almost felt like he was on his way home.

WHAT DO YOU care where they are, Granger?" Marty said. "Are you one of them now too?"

"Hey, didn't I prove myself at Erin's house?" He pushed his bluff. Granger had no one else to turn to. With his ring gone, Marty was his connection to real power.

"Guess you did okay." Marty high-fived Granger.

"All I'm asking is if you know what happened to them. Didn't they teach you anything about religion at the WPA Academy?"

"Yeah, sure. Everything we need to know to keep them at bay. We call 'em *religionists* now, meaning anyone who believes in any kind of religion. We consider them terrorists. Some of them actually believe this rising-from-the-dead stuff. And they have their own books, music, movies, and language. Secret stuff. All the big religions do."

"Molly and Patch said they have a relationship with God. They never used the word *religion*."

"They are the worst type," Marty said. He was in teacher mode. "They think they know everything and everyone is wrong but them."

"So why is the WPA so worried about them?"

"We're not afraid of anything. I'm only helping you to get my chance at your ring."

"Too late," Granger said. "I flushed the thing."

Marty pointed to the door. "Conversation over," he said.

45

So, Patch," Jarrod said, "what's going on with the others?"

Patch shrugged.

Jarrod clomped his crutches out into the field near one of the wooden fences he and Patch had fixed. He turned and stared at Patch thoughtfully.

"What?" Patch asked, following. He felt as though a big target gleamed on his chest.

"Your sister is alive."

"Don't kid about something like that, man."

"I wouldn't! You know me better than that. I saw her."

"Don't do this to me, Jarrod. I mean it." Patch choked back a sob. "You have no idea how much she meant to me."

"Come on. I want to show you something."

Jarrod lurched back to the house and led Patch to the computer on the kitchen table. He found the Web site and Patch stood wide-eyed, watching the video, hearing the familiar voice.

It was Jenny all right. His heart ached to see her, and he breathed a prayer of thanksgiving that beyond hope she'd been saved. But what was all that stuff about Erin? She had kidnapped Jenny and tortured her? He would never believe that, especially after seeing that the video had been posted by the WPA. They never told the truth.

He suddenly understood what treasure Erin had hinted at.

"I've got to find her."

"I'm coming too," Jarrod said.

Sanitizing the tables was their new assignment. But at least they had the cafeteria to themselves. "No. I don't see it," Nancy said. Nothing Molly said could convince her.

"I'm telling you, something about the shape of that kitchen helper's hand reminds me of Claudia."

Nancy had seen that nasty "claw" gesture the old Claudia used to make enough times to recognize the long fingers, the perfect nails. Was Molly on to something? "You're getting pretty desperate if you're longing for Claudia."

Molly looked surprised. "She's changed. We all have."

That made Nancy feel mean. She'd once had a goody-two-shoes reputation. Now she felt positively wicked. "You're right," she said. "Claudia's proved herself."

Molly nodded. "Now what's this big surprise you've got for me?"

"It's my only reason for coming."

She handed a package to Molly, who tore at the tissue covering. Molly gasped.

"You have no idea . . . This is priceless. We can't let anyone see it."

"Well, no kidding!"

"If Lori finds this, they won't just take it away," Molly said. "They'll destroy it."

Suddenly Molly yanked a chunk of pages from the center of the book. Nancy nearly burst into tears.

What in the world was she doing?

She'd given up everything to bring Molly the Bible, and now Molly was ripping it to pieces. Nancy's face warmed. How stupid she'd been to come.

"I know what you went through to get it here," Molly said. "But it's the only way to protect it."

"By destroying it?"

"Not destroying it. Hiding it." Molly sat stripping the Bible into chunks and piling them neatly. "It's our only option. If they find any of it, at least they won't find all of it."

Classic Molly thinking.

Nancy tried to feel better about it. Tried not to think about what she'd gone through to get the book here. Tried not to be angry.

I WISH BARRY was here," McCry said.

You're the only one, Erin thought.

The taping background was light blue, nice and friendly, like a quiet sky.

On a small raised stage about the size of her parents' living room perched a sofa, and next to it an overstuffed chair. "You want to sit here?" Erin said, pointing to the chair.

McCry took a seat, ramrod straight. Erin almost laughed when she shoved the makeup man. Guess she was comfortable with the tough look. She didn't want them to change a thing.

So what if McCry looked like she'd stuck her finger in a light socket? Not Erin's problem.

"So what do you want me to say?"

"You have the script. Stick to it." The woman would be following word for word, line for line.

Erin read the words to herself again. "Image is everything. I'll bet you thought what you saw about me on OpenEyez.com was real. Obviously it's not, or the WPA wouldn't trust me to make the following statement . . ."

Erin couldn't force herself to inject any enthusiasm into the words. Especially when she thought about what she'd gone through at school, at her house. If only the world knew what had happened. Of course, Erin had to wonder if they'd even care.

She continued reading the script. "I'm really just like you, trying to make good grades, trying to find a date for the latest movie. We're really a lot alike, you and I. Just like you, my family means everything to me. That's why I support the WPA . . ."

After someone swiped some blush onto her cheeks and yanked a brush through her hair, Erin found herself sitting before the camera.

McCry motioned to her to sit taller. "And don't forget to pause meaningfully, flip your hair, and smile."

Gag.

The camera rolled and Erin read through the script the best she could, finishing with, "The World Peace Alliance brings hope and honors families because it doesn't put any one belief above another. That's what makes us all equal. That's what makes us human."

The message was clear: support the WPA or you're a traitor.

How long could Erin keep this up? "Are you going to send me home?" She forced herself not to whisper "Please."

McCry smiled wide. "We have a few other projects for you."

"So I'm not free?"

"You never have been."

46

Y UCK. BARRY SMELLED the stink of prayer in Jarrod's house. The man and woman had dropped to their knees the moment the two demons walked through the door.

"Patch was here," he said, searching the kitchen. "And his twisted friend, the crutch king."

"Where'd they go?" Hope's grating whine made Barry grimace.

"Then I guess we ask them again," he said, using his hoof to nudge the couple huddled on the floor.

"Jesus, protect us. Protect those boys," the man's strong voice said.

"Hurry up," Hope said, glugging a gallon of orange juice from the fridge. She tore into a jar of cookies.

"They don't seem willing to help," Barry said. He and Hope had torn off their human skin and were playing trick-or-treat for real.

"We won't tell you a thing," the woman said. Barry raised a clawed fist as if to slap her, and she quieted. The man had not stopped praying since they entered. His words were like ground glass in Barry's ears. But he couldn't do any more than try to scare the lady. And it wasn't working.

If he would only shut up. Barry wanted to terrify these two, but they were not quivering.

And worse: *it* was coming. Barry's fear. The humans' words to the enemy tore Barry apart. Made him cringe and crumble. He hated the stretching in his stomach, the dry clump that was once his brain. Something was destroying him from the inside out.

They had to get out before the couple's prayers sent them back to hell's portal. He refused to end up like Trevor had.

"Don't tell us, then," Barry said. "Fine. You'll regret it." His voice cracked.

Hope growled, cookie crumbs cascading past her craggy chin.

Barry's legs had a life of their own. "We're leaving," he roared, but it came out like a cat's yowl. "We'll find them, and there's nothing you can do to protect them."

If they didn't hurry they'd shrink to insect proportions. Hope finally felt the effects. She held her ears and cried out as she followed Barry. "The prayers. Stop them!"

Outside they pulled their human costumes back on and climbed into the vehicle.

"You were lying," Hope said.

"I know," Barry said. "It's what I do."

But he knew what she meant. If those people kept praying, he and Hope might never find Patrick Johnson. Their stupid prayers were blocking him. They had to find some unholy humans if they wanted to capture their prey.

Barry refused to admit failure.

Doesn't go too fast," Patch said. He didn't want to sound critical. The truck Jarrod's father had provided was the best of the ranch vehicles. The half-ton was theirs as long as they needed it.

"Push the pedal harder. And keep praying."

Patch realized that their escape had far more to do with God's intervention than with this worn-out bucket of bolts. No matter how fast they drove, if they weren't walking in God's will they would fail.

"Your parents are incredible." Patch meant it.

He thought about how Jarrod's mom had donated her laptop—fully loaded, wireless ready. "Might come in handy for keeping a step ahead," she'd said. She had wrapped them some dinner, and—like father like son—Jarrod's dad had pushed more cash into Patch's hand. A lot. And he wouldn't take no for an answer. "You find your little sister."

Patch and Jarrod would start their search in the most logical place. With McCry.

47

ERIN WAS A whacko. When the buzz first hit the school about her holding a kid captive, Granger didn't believe a word. Until he saw the video.

And now a complete flip-flop. Speaking for the WPA? From Christ-Kid to kidnapper?

Didn't make any sense.

"Guess you were wrong about her," Marty had said earlier. "She's no Christian."

"Seems like," Granger said.

"I checked with McCry," Marty said. "It's true. Erin's one of us now."

This was insane. Erin had given up on everything she'd said in Demon's Bluff?

She wasn't the only false one. Thoughts of his own picture brought a lump to Granger's throat. His eyes told him one thing, his heart another. Nothing was certain. He felt as confused as he had that time in Demon's Bluff when everyone needed his help, but he'd turned and run. Shame flooded him.

Granger had hidden when things got tough. He'd refused to take a stand. And he had certainly put no trust in the so-called power of prayer. Then, as now, he'd waited on the sidelines, watching to see how things would unfold.

Once he even tried asking God for help. But nothing happened. At least nothing good. The most horrible memory filled his head: Claudia swinging back and forth on a demon's thrashing tail.

He remembered the night. Erin had screamed at him, "Help her, Granger!"

But instead of being a man, he'd run. Slipped behind a tree. He'd actually told Erin, "No way." The guilt still gnawed at him.

He'd done what he'd done.

At the moment Granger felt like a rat in a maze, sniffing around, confused, holding out for the ultimate chunk of cheese. But what if he'd already seen the Truth and passed on it, hoping for something better?

Clearly the WPA found something scary about Jesus. Why? He had been dead for thousands of years.

Granger hated to admit it, but Patch was the guy he wanted to talk to. And, as before, Marty was his only chance of finding him.

Granger got on his bike and zipped to Marty's house. The guy was tight with McCry. He should have some answers.

"Marty, I know you're high enough in the WPA to know where Patch is."

Marty's chest seemed to expand. "Well, of course I do, but it's confidential." He paused, looking both ways. "I'm not supposed to be saying this, but . . ."

Apparently Marty was drunk with his own importance. He told Granger everything, even that Jarrod was with Patch, probably heading for some desert cave.

THE ROOM WAS beautiful. Thick cushions, a wide-screen TV. Plenty of remotes. The apartment Erin had always dreamed of.

At least it would look nice on screen. But it was a mirage. She lived in a partial house on a sound stage. The refrigerator was full of food, the microwave worked. A bedroom with a rack for clothes hid behind a shell of a wall. A small bathroom was her only private spot. At least she hoped it was.

Her house even had a front door . . . that didn't open.

It was her own place in the middle of a dark warehouse.

"You're free to go anywhere you want," McCry said, smiling. "As long as you stay here."

"What about school?"

"Such a scholar," McCry said. "We'll get you whatever materials you need. Even your tests."

"And my parents?"

"They're fine with this, Erin." The silver-haired woman drew in a deep breath. "And I think you'll find more room to roam here than at the Home."

"Can't I see my little brother?"

"Finish up some film projects, and we'll see what we can work out."

Erin had the ultimate apartment, with loneliness for a roommate.

When McCry finally left, Erin dropped to her knees right in front of the cameras and crew. Let them see her pray.

GRANGER WAS BACK to wondering about the gang and their faith. He sat in algebra class thinking about how they were all gone. Not that they'd ever done anything for him. They were mostly just hypocrites like Erin. Okay, maybe he'd seen some differences in Molly, but Nancy was still a flake. And Claudia . . . Well, she was different, but not really in a good way. She still seemed to think she was always right.

Why would Granger want to be part of something that didn't work? Seemed the WPA brought out true allegiance. And lots of rewards.

If Erin and Marty were in, maybe Granger should give the World Peace Alliance a shot.

He gathered his books and rose.

"Take your seat, Granger." The class stared.

He went to the door. "I don't feel good," he said. "I'm confused." A lame smile crossed his lips.

"That's the least of your problems," the teacher said. "See the nurse."

Granger slipped out, knowing who had the answers—supposedly. He slowed at the WPA recruitment signs on every bulletin board. They paid for college, gave you a car, travel, clothing allowance. And that whole crowd-control thing was a lot of fun. He wanted another hit of the power.

Now that would be cool.

And he had an awesome "in." Marty.

Why not give it a try? Make a solid decision for once.

WHAT IN THE world? Another day, another chance to step in to help those two. Claudia wondered how obvious Molly and Nancy could be. It was like they were hiding Easter eggs, shoving something between boards and into various nooks and crannies.

Claudia also saw Lori hiding behind a trash can, sneaking a cigarette. Molly was getting close, so Claudia knew she had to distract Lori.

"Hey," she said.

Lori drew another lungful, dropping the butt. She looked ready to tear off Claudia's face.

"Spying on me, kitchen klutz?"

"Never. I just figured you're the girl to know," Claudia said, trying to keep Lori's eyes on her.

Lori squinted. "Could be."

"I'm new here."

"No kidding. And uncoordinated."

"That's for sure. But I do like making desserts. I can sneak you some."

The girl was apparently used to people buying her off. "Lead the way," she said.

Claudia snuck her into the kitchen and to the chocolate pudding bowl, filled with enough for dozens. Lori grabbed a serving spoon and dug in like a kid on her first birthday.

"Let me scoop some out for you." Too late. Lori slopped the spoon from her mouth to the mixing bowl. And back. All hers now.

"You're not bad for kitchen help," Lori said with her mouth full.

At least Molly's mission was safe from Lori.

Y OU'RE THE ONE who's going to tell her the details," Hope said. "I'm not the one who messed everything up."

Barry slammed on the brakes of the rental car as they reached the WPA headquarters. He hadn't given Hope any warning, and he laughed as her head almost hit the dashboard. She had frayed his last nerve on the flight home and the trip back to town.

"McCry will hear about that," she said, glaring at him on their way in. Her mask didn't seem quite right. Her eyes looked crooked, her mouth twisted.

"Tell McCry we're coming up," Hope told the receptionist as they headed for the elevator.

"This really is McCry's fault," Barry said.

"Well," Hope said, "she won't be pleased with you. I know I'm not."

Barry mashed the emergency stop button and an alarm sounded.

"What are you doing?"

"You want to have it out right now?" he said. He was sure he could take her. Only one of them could be in charge. If it wasn't going to be him, he'd rather be sent to the other place.

"I was joking," Hope said, not looking at him. "Open the door."

48

WHY HADN'T SHE thought of this before?

Excited, Erin pounded in a number on her cell phone. But no. It wouldn't even ring, let alone roam. It was as if she was trying to call from a tomb.

Web surfing. Texting. All worthless.

She keyed through her address book. At least she had a list of people to pray for.

How could her parents allow this?

The steel door opened. It was McCry, the boss from hell. Her silver eyes looked tired but intense.

"Never again." She slapped some papers down in front of Erin. "Our ranking stinks because *your* presentation was weak. Unconvincing. I won't have that."

"You're critiquing my lies?"

"They're only lies if you don't believe what you're saying. People can see it in your eyes." McCry sat on the couch. "I'm going to motivate you."

Erin reached for the photograph McCry held out. It was her little brother. A sick feeling crept into her throat. "What are you talking about?"

"He'll be okay." McCry snatched the picture and tore it in half. "If you try harder."

THINK ANYONE WILL notice this old beater among the Beemers?" Jarrod patted the console of his dad's truck as they parked at WPA headquarters. They'd finally made it to town after sleeping last night on the truck bed in thin sleeping bags. At least he'd tried to sleep. But whenever he closed his eyes he felt that someone was watching him. Standing over him.

Patch locked his door. "Hope nobody tries to steal it," he said. "It's a classic."

They made their way inside to the reception desk.

"Patrick Johnson to see Cheryl McCry."

The receptionist looked startled. "Is she expecting you?"

"Believe me, she's been hoping for this meeting for quite awhile."

The idea of walking right into McCry territory was gutsy. But Patch felt that he was supposed to. If only he could be sure it was God leading his steps, and not his own willfulness.

The receptionist spoke quietly into the phone, eyes on Patch and his friend. Then, "Ms. McCry will see you now, Mr. Johnson. Alone."

"We're a team," Jarrod said.

She pointed to the bank of elevators. "Fine. Take the middle elevator to the seventh floor."

As they walked away Patch heard the woman quietly call for Security.

BARRY WATCHED McCRY'S face when she took the phone call. Something was up. She'd been the one to call them back to her office, but now she suddenly lost interest in them.

When she hung up, Hope continued. "As I was saying, Ms. McCry, Barry has mishandled this whole case from the beginning. If you took him off . . ." She scratched at her cheek too hard—her mask slipped for a second. She pushed it back into place.

"Neither of you have shown me much initiative." McCry stared at the door.

"It's not my fault," Hope said. "I can be reassigned."

"She certainly can," Barry said. The little traitor didn't deserve to have the benefit of his skill. Let her try on her own and see how she did.

"We went through this earlier. So the trail went cold?" McCry said. "Sloppy work."

"There's enough blame to go around," Barry said. "The enforcers weren't competent."

"Having worked with Trevor, you are certainly experts on incompetence," McCry said. "I make enough mistakes on my own without working with fools like you."

Barry felt like a kid in trouble, not an all-powerful demon. What was wrong? Where was the fear? "Give us another chance," he said, knowing he sounded pathetic. This would not look good back at the office. Demons weren't fired.

McCry shook her head. She was no longer impressed.

"But you still haven't caught Johnson," Hope said.

There was a knock at the door. Barry smelled him before he saw him.

"It's open," McCry said.

Patch.

"Afternoon, Ms. McCry," he said. "I'd appreciate a few moments. You remember Jarrod."

"Certainly," McCry said. She extended a hand as if meeting old friends. "He probably considers me the foulest of all sinners." She pinned Patch with a grin. "Just like you."

"I'd be willing to arm wrestle you for the title," Jarrod said.

McCry snorted.

Just like that, Barry and Hope were out of the equation.

Jenny had never felt so alone. A big burly man shoved her when she stood too long in the hallway.

"Don't block other kids," he said. He didn't smile. She wondered if he could.

Jenny tramped into the playroom. Lots of tiny tables made for just one child. Comfortable video chairs for hooking into the TV or playing a game.

Jenny wanted to make friends, but angry faces glared when she tried. She was so lonely.

She tapped a young girl on her shoulder and asked how she was today. An adult along the wall jumped between them, shaking a finger in her face. "Go find a puzzle or video game. Stay out of trouble."

Jenny got bored quickly. She wished someone would read her a book—like Erin used to. But there weren't any stories around.

Green flashing lights at the edges of the doorway told Jenny it was time for the next activity. Lunch.

She sat next to the girl from the game room but didn't dare whisper hello. She stared down at her food, pushing peas with her fork, then popped them into her mouth one at a time. Another quiet meal.

More flashing green lights. Time for the movie room. Something about wildlife again.

Jenny longed to be outdoors. To play hide-and-seek. Anything.

The Peaceful One watched the child. He wanted to speak to her but was forbidden any contact. The child had to wait.

So did he. His only hope was that Jenny had spent enough time with Erin that she learned something about prayer. About hope.

No matter how many children he'd guarded, he knew that God's timing must always be heeded. His wisdom never failed.

If only Jenny could understand.

Y OU PICKED AN awesome day to join the WPA," Marty said. Granger couldn't remember seeing his friend so happy, like he'd had a chocolate shake for breakfast.

"What happened, man?" Granger could tell something was up. Maybe this wasn't such a good idea after all.

"The freak turned himself in. Patch. He dragged along some guy on crutches, not exactly who I'd have picked in battle."

Granger knew Jarrod. He had prayed with him once upon a time. Now he was ready to join the WPA—the organization trying to capture his old friend.

"Why in the world would Patch do that?" Granger wanted to know—really wanted to understand. For the life of him, the Christ-Kids didn't make sense. They were always doing exactly the opposite of what seemed best for them.

"He's stupid," Marty said. "He thinks confessing his sins will get him in good with McCry and give him a chance to see his sister."

That made sense. "Think it'll work?"

"With McCry?" Marty made a face and shook his head. "She's already moved the kid."

"Patch doesn't know that?"

"Of course not." Marty made a threatening gesture. "And anyone connected with the WPA will keep his mouth shut too."

"Right," Granger said, slipping his hands behind his back. "Definitely."

49

PATCH STOOD, STUNNED. Jarrod's mouth was open, too, staring at the woman.

"I can't explain it any more clearly," McCry said. "We don't need you anymore. We have Erin. She's calm. Smart. Never says too much or too little." McCry piled folders into a stack. "And unlike you, people actually like her."

"She's doing this of her own free will?" Jarrod said.

McCry stood. "Do any of us ever do anything we don't have to?"

"You're blackmailing her, aren't you?" Patch said. "Like you wanted to do with me and Jenny."

"You know," McCry said, "it just doesn't matter anymore. Crawl back under the rock you call home. Both of you."

"I want to see my sister."

"She'll be fine if you promise to stay away from her."

Patch realized McCry had found a new way to hurt him more than she'd ever hurt him before—by keeping him from his sister. And she knew it too. Knew the pain she caused.

"You're nothing to me. To any of us." McCry crossed her arms and stood before Patch. "You have no information I need. You're worthless." She pointed at Jarrod. "You make quite a pair."

"I have to find Jenny." Patch dropped to his knees. He was willing to beg, do anything. His sister needed him. And he needed her.

"An escort downstairs," McCry said into her intercom. When the two toughs arrived, she told them, "If they're spotted again, shoot them." Patch's last image was the sick sight of McCry's smile.

It HAD BEEN less than a week, but Erin hated her life already. She got assignments from both school and the WPA. Writing presentations, speech preparation, a daily blog.

McCry forced her to say what they wanted her to say, constantly holding over her head the chance to see Terry again. But she had made a solemn promise to God. She would not say anything that would even hint that she didn't believe in Jesus. She could babble on all they wanted about tolerance and getting along, but no way would she say anything bad about God.

Most of the comments on her blog were filled with perky psychobabble from people glad she was back in the fold, aligned with the WPA.

But one caught her eye: The Fish Guy. It was a short plea. "Family is important to me, friend," it said. "Where is she?"

She pictured the small fish tattoo that Patch had gotten on his ankle when he'd joined the Tattooed Rats, as a secret sign for other Christians.

Could this really be Patch? Erin wanted to help him, but couldn't. Not without endangering Terry.

Or could she?

"The home is one of the most important places for a child to feel safe," Erin began. As she typed, the words flowed. She wrote that the house wasn't just a place where families gathered and said hello to each other between activities. A real home was a place where people cared for each other . . .

IT'S HUMILIATING," HOPE said. "We can't be demoted. McCry won't get away with this."

"Already has," Barry said. "We lost this one."

"What about Marty?"

"The guy was sure attracted to you," Barry said. "He liked you as much as he hated me."

"He's got good taste."

Idiot. Hope sounded more human every day.

"I still want Patch," Barry said. The guy had shamed him.

"Me too," Hope said. "But we're sharing the reward."

NANCY WRUNG HER hands. Molly wished she would stop. "I know you want out, but it's not time."

At least they could keep an eye on Claudia. If it was really her. And if it was, she had really changed.

"I want to go home, is all," Nancy said. "I came here to give you the Bible and tell you I was sorry for everything I've done. But this place is horrible. I just want to get back to my own room—any place that doesn't have Lori."

"I think God has other plans," Molly said. "But fine, if you want to leave, I'll help. And maybe Claudia can help too." Molly hoped Claudia could persuade Nancy to be more patient.

PATCH READ AND reread Erin's blog about home. He and Jarrod sat on the truck tailgate at the city park.

"Maybe she didn't get that it was from you," Jarrod said.

"She had to. I'm just trying to figure out what she's trying to tell me."

Patch hated the WPA babble-speak she was required to use. The big question, though, was whether he could even trust her. What if she really had turned?

"What about sending another message?" Jarrod said. "Something less subtle."

They leaned over the laptop and linked to Erin's blog.

"I'm missing something," Patch wrote. "Tell me more about home."

I'LL TELL McCRY you're here," Marty said.

Granger nodded and gave a cheery thumbs-up, trying to convince himself as much as Marty. The WPA would provide some structure. And extra spending money.

He told himself to forget about Patch and not worry about Jarrod. But he couldn't. That summer thing at Demon's Bluff hadn't been all hype. And hadn't he faced down a monster for Nancy?

He felt a sudden need for fresh air. He could check with Marty later about signing up for the WPA. For now he had to get out.

He rushed outside and was buckling himself into his car when he noticed her sitting in the passenger seat.

"Hope?" He knew he sounded stupid. She put her hand on his.

"There was a rumor about you," she said, her voice low.

Granger was baffled. "Me?"

"Heard you had feelings for someone." Hope chewed a strand of hair.

Yes, he did. And how could this beautiful girl have anything to do with Barry? She needed his protection. Like Nancy did.

Hope winked at him.

"Yeah, I kind of like you," Granger said.

"Ahh."

Hope smiled. He watched as she reached behind her head, and then he felt a sudden, unexpected dread.

The next second her head flipped back like an opening trash can and she swung a gnarled fist into his shoulder, needlelike nails biting into his skin.

Granger shrieked.

"Love hurts," Hope said, laughing.

50

ERIN'S SPIRIT TOLD her the message was from Patch. But he sounded so worried. Erin wished she was still at the Home with Jenny instead of trapped in a fake house.

"Ask Mom," Erin typed as her title. Then she wrote:

One thing I've discovered as I creep toward 20 (in a few years), is that Mom knows more than I gave her credit for even a few years ago. She has experienced more than I imagine. She has the answers to questions I'm sometimes afraid to ask. Reasons I don't agree with but that make sense to her . . .

And so I say again, ask Mom.

She couldn't be any clearer without getting in huge trouble.

Another wise, down-home column for the world, but really written for Patch. *Please read between the lines*, Erin prayed.

CLAUDIA PULLED OFF her tacky hairnet, her blond hair curly in the humid kitchen. "Okay, so it wasn't much of a disguise," she said. She hugged her friends.

Nancy immediately talked of escape. "I know I can make things right again with my mom." All she worried about was herself.

"You might be able to sneak her out, Claudia," Molly said. "But I don't want to put you in danger."

"I've been thinking about this. I'm an employee," Claudia said. "I can stay or leave when my shift is over. No big deal. No one cares."

"So I can go with you?" Nancy said.

Molly gave her a look. "How's your mom?"

Claudia suddenly teared up. "Haven't heard a word for days. Hope was going to take care of things for me." She wiped her eyes.

"We'll keep praying," Molly said.

"So—about me leaving." Nancy tapped her foot.

"Maybe," Claudia said. "But if we get caught, we're both in trouble."

Claudia raised an eyebrow. "You coming, too, Molly?"

"No. These girls need Jesus."

LAST NIGHT JENNY had dreamed about the angel again. The strong one with the kind face. When she woke she peeked behind the curtains to see if he was still around.

She wished she could stay in bed all day. But the smell of frying eggs and buttery toast made her hungry.

She dressed and joined the other children marching slowly past her door.

The angel's smile made Jenny feel better. But he was only a dream. She wanted somebody real by her side. Like Mommy or Daddy. Or Patchy. It was hard to believe they were all gone. And what about Terry's sister, Erin?

Erin talked about Jesus and said she could pray to him for help. She'd have to try that.

51

ERIN COULD ONLY hope Patch had understood her message this time. He had to. If she was caught being more specific, the WPA might move Jenny again making it even tougher for Patch to find her.

But she hadn't gotten a response yet to yesterday's comments. She wondered if McCry had gotten him.

"Hello, Erin."

Speak of the devil.

"You don't knock?" Erin said, finishing her cereal.

McCry snorted. "Not in my job description. Hey, lots of good comments on your blog."

That was all she needed, compliments from the enemy.

"Thanks."

McCry let a smile crawl across her face. "You tried to trick us."

Erin raised her arms in mock surrender. "Can't pull anything over on you."

"'The Fish Guy'? Did Johnson actually think I'd miss that mark when we had him in custody?"

They knew about the tattoo? How did they always know? Goose flesh rose on Erin's arms.

"You're not my target audience," Erin said icily.

"Just know we're watching, and don't try it again."

Hmm. No mention of the second message, the one about her mom. Maybe McCry wasn't so swift. Or maybe Erin's prayers that certain eyes would be blinded were being answered.

Aₙₒₜₕₑᵣ

ANOTHER MORNING, ANOTHER tedious discussion. "You think I'm a bad person, don't you, Molly?"

Why did Nancy allow the devil to terrify her?

"Nancy, if God wants you to go back home—" She wanted to put this kindly. Lately she'd been letting her mouth run off with her. "—You need to do what God wants you to."

"Wish I could be brave like you and Claudia."

"You were brave to come. Well, God can use you as you are." Molly helped Nancy stuff her few belongings into two cheap plastic grocery bags so she'd look like she was taking out the trash, not trying to leave.

"I've never been an upfront kind of person," Nancy said. "I like being behind the scenes."

"Go back. Pray for people. Live the truth in your life."

Nancy seemed to be considering. "You don't think I'm a coward?"

"I care about you, Nancy. Even though you think different, act different, do everything opposite to the way I would." Molly hugged her.

PATCH ALMOST THREW up. First being kicked out of McCry's office, and now this. He shoved the laptop toward Jarrod. "She's sick."

How could Erin be so cruel? She knew he couldn't ask his mom anything. She was dead. All he had left was Jenny. He had to find her.

"Ask Mom." The words stung.

Jarrod slapped the lid down. "Get over yourself," he said and pushed Patch off the tailgate. He hit the ground hard.

"What's that about?" Now he was angry at Jarrod and Erin.

Jarrod gently clunked Patch on the skull with his knuckle. "She's not talking about *your* mother. She's giving you a clue. Remember, you're not the only one on the planet reading her blog. She's talking about Mrs. Morgan, her own mom. She knows something about Jenny."

Of course! How could he have been so stupid? "Man, you're right, as usual. And I'm an idiot. Let's go."

Patch packed up his equipment while Jarrod hobbled to the truck. Patch was right behind him. In minutes they were at Erin's house.

Patch was surprised at the emotions that went through him. Here is where his journey with his friends had begun. Here is where he'd first met Erin. The thought brought a smile to his face.

But the thought of seeing Erin's parents brought a bad taste to his mouth. The relationship between him and them had been rocky at best. Especially with Mrs. Morgan. The idea of seeing her sent chills down Patch's spine. He did not trust her.

But Erin had hinted that somehow she was the key to finding his sister.

He and Jarrod mounted the steps and rang the bell. Mrs. Morgan opened the door just enough to see who it was.

"You're not welcome here. Never have been."

A familiar face tried to squeeze between his mom's knees. Terry. "Patchy! You're back!"

He squirmed through like a puppy beneath a fence and leaped into Patch's arms. Patch hugged him tightly.

"Are you still the coolest kid on the block, little guy?"

The boy's grin would not stop. "Mommy, Patchy is back!"

"McCry told me that if you tried to see your sister I was to restrain you," Mrs. Morgan said.

Patch and Jarrod exchanged looks. Jarrod said, "We're not afraid."

"You have to tell me about Jenny," Patch said. "Where is she?"

"I don't know what—"

"Who?" Terry said.

"My sister, Jenny," Patch said. He scruffed the boy's hair. "You'd like her. She's smart like you."

"She's my friend!" Terry said. "She used to live with us."

Mrs. Morgan's arms were tightly entwined. The boy must be telling the truth.

"Please help me," Patch said. "Tell me."

"I can't."

"Erin said I could come to you, that you would have the answers."

Mrs. Morgan stiffened. "Erin actually said something nice about me?"

"She loves you."

The woman's hard expression wavered. "Don't you throw the word *love* around. Erin disagrees with every decision I've ever made." She put a hand on the porch railing. "I'm always wrong." Her chin quivered.

"Is it possible that sometimes you *are* wrong?" Jarrod said.

She rubbed her neck and shook her head. "I can't help you. There's no telling what McCry would do." She seemed to be struggling with something.

"Patchy's sister needs him," Terry said. "Like I miss Erin."

At the sincerity in Terry's voice, Patch felt tears spring to his eyes. He looked at Erin's mom and prayed with all his heart that she'd understand.

And Mrs. Morgan broke. She spoke quickly, eyes flitting. "It's called the Home, and it's not far . . ."

52

BARRY HATED HOPE as much as he needed her.

She had a way of weaseling information out of these foolish humans. Her charms worked.

They had to get Patch before McCry did. It was a matter of honor. Even if he hated Trevor, the two were demons under the skin. They owed it to him. To their supervisor, Flabbygums. To all of their associates in the netherworld.

Barry shrank down to bug size and buzzed past a McDonald's restaurant. He much preferred super stature, but he didn't really have a choice. If he didn't drum up some real fear, he'd stay shrimpy. The idea of remaining for much longer in this weak human world gave him the shivers.

THE THREE OF them stood in the industrial kitchen, chewing chocolate chips.

"That's all there is to it?" Nancy said.

"Not everything has to be complicated," Claudia said.

Molly agreed. Tonight Claudia would roll out the large trash bins behind the building. Nancy would hide inside, covered with old sacks and maybe some gunk.

"Yuck! Couldn't I just sneak out after the meal?"

"This is safest for both you and Claudia."

"I can't believe you both want to stay in this place," Nancy said. "I don't ever want to see it again."

She heard something. Had someone been listening?

Lori sauntered in. "So, is this party private?" She held out her hand. Without hesitation, Claudia filled it with chips.

"So, what's this about big plans for tonight?"

"Oh yeah," Claudia said. "Big plans. Humongous." She gestured for Lori to come closer.

"Is it a secret?" Lori said.

"Like everything worth knowing. But you'd better not let anything slip to Miss Grady."

"So what's the scam?"

"Prison break," Claudia said.

Claudia ignored Molly's double take.

"Cool," Lori said. "How?"

"Tunnels. You know those little plastic spoons that come with the *el cheapo* ice cream sundaes?"

"The ones where you pop off that white cardboard top?" Lori said.

"We've been saving those little spoons. Lots of them. Dozens of them. Maybe more. We figure we only have to eat a few more tons until we have enough."

Lori laughed. "So you don't trust me?"

"Nope," Claudia said. Beautifully blunt, Molly thought.

"That's okay," Lori said. "Long as you keep the chocolate coming, you can get by with anything."

EVERY DAY BROUGHT another broadcast. Erin felt sick being phony on camera. Just like always. But she couldn't rebel. Not yet. Not until she knew Terry was okay.

She could have come clean immediately and gone down in flames for claiming Christ. But what good would that have done? She'd never have been able to help Patch.

Erin's Corner was the gaggy name McCry had came up with for her show. Hokey, but people tuned in.

For the umpteenth time Erin mentioned how much she cared about her young brother. She refused to give his name so he'd have some privacy.

Today it was another interview with McCry, who herself still seemed awkward on camera. "You realize there is more than one truth," McCry said, her face a gentle mask.

"I'm not sure we need more than one," Erin said. "If there *is* more than one, doesn't all truth disappear? Or blend into meaninglessness?"

"You sound religious, Erin." McCry leaned in, apparently pretending to be some famous interviewer.

"Religious?" This was too easy. "Absolutely not. Being religious means doing things for the sake of earning some favor, not because you trust in an underlying truth."

"Back to that truth trouble again, are we?" McCry said, laughing weakly.

It sounded so phony. Why did it cut to Erin's heart?

"I guess so, ma'am." She forced her smile wider. "Truth is the only thing that matters," she said.

"After the commercial break you can tell us your definition of *truth*," McCry said.

53

Y ou and Barry." Granger gasped. "You're both like him." He panted like an old dog.

"Who, Trevor? Actually, I think you mean like 'it.'" Granger's terror made Hope happy—at least as pleased as a demon could be.

"I thought we had something going." Granger squirmed to get out of her grasp.

She smelled sweat. That scent would attract Barry.

A buzzing insect flitted past. It landed and swelled to demon form. "Save some for me," Barry said. He looked pumped, blood red and slobbering. No more costumes, no more games.

"Leave me in peace," Granger whined.

Hope let him take a couple of steps, then batted him to the ground. "*Peace* is one word I despise," she said.

Granger kept moving, on his knees, an inch at a time.

"Leave him alone," Barry said. "It's disgusting when you play with your food."

Hope swung her tail and smashed Granger into a tree. He fell unconscious. "You're right," she said. "Let's find our real prey and finish this."

Hurry!" Patch banged his hand on the dashboard. He wasn't angry at Jarrod, just at the slow truck. And now they were lost.

"Sorry, but I've never been here before." Jarrod pursed his lips in concentration.

"Let me drive. I've got to get to her before McCry does."

Tonight was the night. As Claudia rolled Nancy out the door with the trash, Molly dropped to her knees. She could hear Claudia talking to the man at the gatehouse. Small talk. And then the sound of her car driving away.

She leaned on her hands, her prayers flowing.

"On your knees again?" Molly saw Lori stick out her tongue.

As she got to her feet, Molly said, "Know what? I can also pray standing, riding a bike, eating hot dogs, and in the shower."

"You really believe it works?"

"Well, it's not about finding a genie and getting your wish."

"So what's the point?"

"Finding out what God wants me to do."

"Who cares?"

"So what matters to you, Lori?"

"My dad used to pray."

Molly wondered if he could have been a secret believer.

"Did you pray with him?"

"All the time." Lori blinked. "Until he died of cancer. He tried everything. Meds, chemo, alternative treatments. Nothing worked." Lori looked out the window. "Somebody suggested prayer. Didn't work either."

"Prayer is not a magic potion," Molly said. "Sometimes God heals. Sometimes he doesn't. He wants us to trust him regardless."

"That's not easy."

"God is God. His plans often differ from mine. That's why I pray so much. I want to know him better and understand his plans for me."

Lori looked uncomfortable. "You ever pray for people who, ah . . . people who aren't your friends?"

"All the time. I pray for you a lot, if that's what you're asking."

54

T HE BREAK WAS over. The producer smiled and said, "You're live in 5–4–3–2 . . ." She held up one finger and Erin welcomed the viewers back. McCry's silver hair stuck up like a crown. Erin noticed that during the break the makeup people kept their distance. She'd scared them one time too many.

"So there's no way to decide which religion is best, right?" McCry squinted.

Erin was supposed to say, "Of course not. We should reject them all."

The cameras whirred. Millions watched.

It's time. Speak now, Erin.

She was ready to obey. *What do I say, God?*

"It's important that we acknowledge there is a spiritual world."

McCry's eyes went cold as she forced a laugh. "You can *acknowledge* all you want. That doesn't make it true."

"What is truth?" Erin stared.

McCry grew quiet. "That's the point. We all have different definitions. Everyone knows that."

"What's yours?" Erin asked.

"This isn't about me."

"Sure it is. If we all have different definitions, I'm sure our viewers would be interested in yours."

"Fine. The truth is what I decide it to be."

"And you've never seen angels or demons? Never witnessed any evidence of a world beyond this one?" Erin swirled her hands.

"Of course not." McCry's eyes darted.

"Ever been to a place called Demon's Bluff?" If it was time, then she had to go through with it—no matter what the consequences.

McCry squirmed. "I'm not at liberty to discuss my assignments. And neither are you."

"Everything's on the table when we talk about truth, isn't it, Ms. McCry?" Erin nodded to a young male production assistant—a big fan who thought McCry was too bossy. Erin had told the man she'd prepared a little surprise for McCry. The guy hadn't asked any questions, just taken the video clip and said that all Erin had to do was nod his way.

Erin made a quick introduction. "Here's an exclusive video our audience might find interesting. I certainly do."

The clip showed McCry talking to Molly and Claudia while clutching Patch's neck. The boy stumbled and landed hard on his knees.

"So you get half and we split the other half?" Claudia said.

"The paperwork will show that the whole reward goes to you," McCry said.

"Because you can't collect the money yourself," Molly said.

Patch pulled himself to his feet.

"If you want to be crude about it," McCry said, "yes."

Claudia patted Patch on the chest. "We just want to be clear."

"Yes," Molly said. "I think Ms. Frazier will find this crystal clear."

So there was McCry on tape offering to break the law, to steal money from the WPA. The video ended with a furious McCry turning away.

McCry stood and swore before realizing the cameras were still rolling. "You little scum!" She jammed a finger in Erin's face and the place exploded with her shouts. "You're finished! Get out of here!"

Erin smiled. Free. She could see Terry, work things out with her parents, find Patch.

But before she could flee, McCry grabbed her by the shoulders. "You'll find out what it's like to survive on your ideals." She squeezed Erin so hard it hurt. "You can't go home, can't attend school." She spat on the floor. "You'll be living on the streets."

Erin hadn't seen how bleak the picture was. But God would protect her.

He had to.

SOMEONE, SOMEHOW, SPOKE to Molly. Maybe it was an angel whispering in her ear.

Claudia and Nancy were safe. Their escape was an answer to prayer. Molly had no idea what God had in store for the two of them. Perhaps her story would intersect with theirs again. Maybe not.

For now, she knew what God wanted her to do. Stay at Straight Arrow indefinitely. But that was okay. Lori needed her. More than that, Lori needed Jesus.

And Molly would tell her about him. About the prayers he had answered.

And the ones denied.

She would tell her the truth.

GRAY CLOUDS HUNG in the night sky. No stars. They'd already missed the regular visitor hours. So what? Nothing was going to stop him. Patch ignored the "No Guests without Appointment" sign and stomped to the front door, holding it open for Jarrod. Before they reached the front desk, a burly orderly dug a fist into his chest.

"No outsiders allowed." His teeth gleamed white. "Too late. Can't you read?" He pointed to the posted hours.

"I'm family. Isn't it good for the children to see their siblings?" Patch struggled to stay calm.

The orderly moved to the front desk. "Who did you want to see?"

"Jenna Johnson." Patch hadn't used her real name in years.

The orderly typed something into the computer. He looked irritated. "Her visitor status is listed as 'restricted,' and it also says she has no blood relatives." The man pursed his lips.

"I'm her brother. Our parents were killed."

"Do you have any ID?" the man said.

Patch yanked his camera memory stick from his pocket. "This shows me with my sister."

If the man confiscated or destroyed this, all evidence of his family would disappear.

The man popped the stick into the computer and waved Patch and Jarrod around the desk.

The machine whirred, and suddenly there was his family on screen, thumbnails of Jenny at her birthday, during Christmas, sitting with Patch. Happy faces, lots of hugs.

The "before" pictures. Before the killing began.

He pointed to one. The man magnified it.

Patch had trouble breathing.

The photo showed Jenny on his lap, her face messy from a fresh peach. "That's her."

"I've seen her," the orderly said. "Some older, but I'm pretty sure it's the same girl." His voice had softened.

"Could you get her, please?"

"My supervisor should be here in a minute."

Not good. Patch waited. As if on cue, the phone rang. The

orderly answered, and Patch saw a change in his face. "Yeah, he's here, and I'm sure he's her brother . . ." He turned and lowered his voice. "He's not going to be happy."

Patch's stomach churned. So close.

"Come with me," the orderly said, avoiding Patch's eye. "Papers to sign first."

Why should that make him unhappy? Though the man returned the memory stick, Patch knew he was lying.

Before he could say anything, the plate glass windows on either side of the front door shattered simultaneously. Patch threw his hands over his face as the shards skittered. Jarrod hit the ground.

Hope and Barry. No more disguises.

Demon Girl flicked her tail and wrapped it around Patch's leg. The orderly dove behind the counter.

"We don't want you," Barry said. The man scurried away.

Hope pulled Patch closer and flipped him upside down, head inches from the floor.

"Take me instead," Jarrod said, crutching his way to Barry.

"We don't deal in rejects." Barry pounded Jarrod with a clawed fist.

"I'm no reject to God," Jarrod said.

"Arguing with us is *such* a waste of time," Hope said. "But fine, we'll take you both. Might be half a reward for you."

Patch was thinking only of Jenny. Let these monsters haul them away if that kept her safe.

"We can't read *your* mind," Barry said. "Fortunately, the orderly was an open book."

They knew. "Take me."

"Thought you wanted to see your sister," Hope said. "Our goal is to make hell one big family reunion."

"Forget about her. Let's go," Patch said.

But Hope smiled.

He twisted his head to see where she was looking. Another orderly stood at the door, holding Jenny's hand. She looked terrified but still she ran to him. "Patchy! You're alive! You came for me!"

Hope let him fall and his head banged on the floor. But all he felt was his sister's thin arms wrapped around his neck.

"What a putrid picture," Hope said.

"She doesn't have any idea what we do to children," Barry said.

Patch knew he could do nothing to protect her.

Except pray.

As a demon grabbed Jenny, Patch cried out, "God, help us!" Hope froze, her clawed arm squeezing the child tight. Her huge craggy eyes blinked, her slobbering mouth moved, but she didn't take another step.

Jenny squirmed but couldn't break free.

"Relax, sweetie," Patch said. He swallowed and looked toward his captor. Barry had him in a similar clasp. One arm digging into his shoulder, the other frozen in time and space. Barry couldn't even twitch his tail.

Jarrod tried to pry Patch and then Jenny free. No good. The creatures clung tight. Something was preventing them from escaping. But the same force kept the demons from doing further damage.

Patch took a deep breath but didn't stop praying.

It was going to be a long night.

THE SHINING ONE stared. He didn't have a single finger on Hope, but she stood stiff with fear. He sensed it. The Radiant One and the Peaceful One surrounded Barry. He knew what they were thinking. He had the same thoughts.

Let us at them, Lord.

But they could only awe the beasts with their source of power. As much as the Shining One wanted to untwine Hope's claw, he had to wait.

The demons were too terrified to move. They hardly breathed. Jenny was all right, for now.

All three angels wondered what order might come next. Until then, they kept the points of their swords inches from the throats of the wicked ones.

55

GOOD THING MCCRY had ranted and walked out last night *before* checking on Erin's status. Erin had been surprised when a sympathetic producer told her to get a good night's rest before leaving. "What could it hurt?" the woman said.

What indeed? Better to at least sleep in a bed before hitting the road tomorrow morning. Especially since she had no idea where she'd go from here.

Erin had tried to pray on her bed, but soon everything went dark. Alone in the studio bedroom, she gave up and went to sleep.

Things still looked bleak in the morning. If she was honest with herself, McCry was right. Unless Erin could work things out with her family, she'd be living out of her car. Jobless. Homeless. Utterly alone. How would she survive?

Erin squinted against the sun as she rolled her suitcase into the parking lot. Time to head home.

If she had one. Of course she wanted to see Terry, but what about Patch?

She wasn't sure if he'd pieced her clues together.

Erin couldn't very well ask her mom the latest on Patch. *Maybe I should just drive by the Home first.* See if she could catch a glimpse of Jenny.

Erin sat in her car and prayed.

The answer came. Yes. She was supposed to visit the Home. Something was happening there. And she was a part of it. She wasn't sure the "something" was good, but she knew she had to get there. Fast. She put the car into gear.

When she got to the Home, she saw the jagged holes in the plate-glass windows. Oh, yeah. She knew she was in the right place. She nosed the car into the nearest spot.

Maybe Patch and Jenny had already escaped. Who knew, though. Especially if the creeps from hell had arrived. But no way was she going to stand there and do nothing. Not if she could help.

Speaking of which, she heard a siren. A WPA car had arrived. She saw McCry's grim grin as the car came closer. And closer. McCry was aiming right for her, obviously wanting a game of Chicken.

Well, fine, Erin could play that game too. She walked to the center of the street, determined not to show fear. She was not going to run. Maybe an accident would slow McCry down.

Erin faced McCry's car and waited. She swallowed. The woman's eyes glinted like polished steel. The car came closer. Erin could see McCry's sneer. Again the car come closer. But at the last moment McCry cranked the wheel. The car swerved, spitting dirt at Erin, and stopped inches away.

"Good driving," Erin said as McCry emerged.

"Weren't you welcome at home?" McCry slammed the door. "Don't worry. Your car will be real comfortable at night—and safe. If there's anything I can do, please hesitate to call."

Erin ignored the dig. "Wanted to check on a friend first." She held the front door open for McCry. They stepped over scattered shards of glass.

McCry stood, hands balled against her sides, surveying the mess. She said, "Don't delude yourself. You don't have any friends."

Erin saw the demons. Turning to McCry, she said, "You're right. Those two are all yours."

Then Erin saw who else was there: Jarrod, standing next to a large counter leaning on his crutches. He looked exhausted. And there was Patch, swaying upside down in the clutches of one demon. Jenny hung enfolded in the tail of the other. When she saw Erin, the child hollered. Erin was afraid for the girl. One slip and she'd crack her head open, break a limb.

McCry marched over as if she had orchestrated the whole event. Maybe she had.

"Put her down," Erin yelled at the demon formerly known as Hope.

The thing shuddered and spat. The girl reached out her hands to Erin.

56

SOMETHING POKED GRANGER. Ouch. That hurt. Hope sure packed a wallop. He'd been out all night.

He pried open his eyes. The Claw?

"Get up."

Nancy stood by her side. Another on the short list of faces he'd rather not see immediately upon awakening.

"Did you close your eyes and run toward the trees?" Nancy said.

"What are you doing here?" Granger let them help him to his feet. "How did you find me?"

"We weren't looking for you," Claudia said. "We've been driving for hours. I saw a blob and thought it was a hurt animal."

"Hope is a demon." He had to get that out.

"Big shock," Nancy said. She wore an I-told-you-so expression.

"Barry too." Granger rubbed his head. "They went after Patch."

"Which way?" Claudia guided him to the car.

Granger pointed to the sky. "They weren't walking. But they have to know he's looking for his sister."

"Who?" Nancy said.

"She's alive. Stayed with Erin for a while. Some big scandal and the WPA took the girl to the Home. Marty told me everything."

"Know where it is?" Claudia said.

"Sure. Marty showed me."

"Get in the car."

WHATEVER INVISIBLE POWER that had kept the demons stilled slipped away. The angry creatures stomped their feet, rolled their shoulders as if they'd just finished a wrestling match. McCry put her hard hand on Patch's shoulder. "You can hand him over now."

Was she blind? Or stupidly brave? Erin saw the way McCry treated these creatures as coworkers, apparently not a bit fazed by their breath or snapping teeth. Guess they were all cut from the same cloth.

Or the woman was a great bluffer.

"He's ours," Barry said, heaving a gust of air. He shook himself like a mutt after a bath.

"He's mine," McCry said.

"You let me go!" Patch said.

"I let you leave town." She swung Patch like a pendulum. Erin cringed. "You disobeyed. I could have you shot."

"Leave Patchy alone!" Jenny screamed. The woman ignored the child. Erin wanted to go to the girl but knew she'd never make it.

"I want the head of the WPA to understand exactly why I've invested so much energy trying to clear out your rat nests of Christ-Kids." McCry jolted Patch to a stop. Erin could see how dizzy he was getting.

Hope stretched her bulging, horned neck. She sniffed at McCry's words. "Our boss is infinitely more demanding," she said. "Besides, you have no authority here."

"Keep the girl." McCry sounded desperate. "I don't care about her."

Maybe she didn't have everything under control, Erin thought.

Patch tried to free himself and Jarrod shuffled over to help. Barry splintered a crutch on him.

"So are you praying, Erin?" McCry whispered.

Erin couldn't believe her ears. Was the woman serious? "I'm going to now," Erin said. Classic McCry. Playing both sides against the middle.

"When will it start working?" McCry's face was lit with desperation.

"We've been given the go-ahead to take these souls," Barry said. "Nothing you can do."

"Jesus." Erin prayed.

The demon flinched and nearly dropped Patch. Why had she waited so long to ask for God's help? Why was she standing and staring?

Erin dropped to her knees.

CLAUDIA RAN THROUGH the shattered front entrance of the Home, followed by Granger and Nancy. The scene that met them was incredible. Barry and Hope weren't cool teens; they were fully stoked demons, and they held Patch and Jenny captive. Jarrod lay on the floor, with Erin nearby. McCry stood helpless while several timid workers from the Home looked on in shock.

Erin felt no surprise at seeing the gang there. God must be in this. "Hurry!" she said. "Pray with me!"

Claudia took her hand. They pushed a pile of glass away, then dropped to their knees next to her.

"Nancy, Granger," Claudia said, "you in or out?"

"I don't believe that stuff," Granger said.

"Yeah," Nancy said, "like demons don't exist." She dropped to the ground. "Jesus, protect them. Protect us."

"How?" Granger said.

"Believe," Erin said. "Admit you're a sinner, that you need Jesus. Accept his forgiveness."

Granger joined the circle. Claudia took his hand.

Erin saw out of the corner of her eye that McCry had slunk closer to the demons.

FREEDOM. THAT WAS all Patch wanted. Freedom for each of them.

His friends were here, and it helped to have them so close. But this wasn't what he'd hoped for. He had seriously thought Jarrod could help him get Jenny and go.

Nothing ever turned out as simply as he wanted.

Would angels intervene this time like they had at Demon's Bluff? Had they already? Is that why the demons had been immovable throughout the night? Or were Patch and his friends on their own? He hoped not.

"God, rescue us!" he cried. "Help us, Jesus!" His fervent prayers left him panting. He could tell they had affected Barry and Hope, but the demons still managed to hold strong.

McCry neared him, her face angry and desperate. "Give him to me!" she screamed suddenly at the monsters. Patch dangled like a toy before a lazy cat.

With the back of a curled claw Barry flicked McCry away, and she rolled like dry tumbleweed.

"Let's take them home," Hope said.

Patch twisted.

Be still. He heard the words loud in his ear. Something was going to happen. Help was coming. He stopped struggling.

Erin stepped forward.

THE SHINING ONE stood watching. The Radiant One and the Peaceful One waited, arms crossed. The boy, his sister, their friends. They needed help.

With a clasp of his hand, the Shining One could destroy a demon.

But the time was not yet.

He sighed.

57

HAD ERIN HEARD right?

Move. Now's the time. Act now!

She wasn't sure what to do. But clearly, God didn't want her standing around.

Someone else had already moved into action. Taking advantage of the lull, McCry was firing orders. She motioned a home worker toward Erin. "Get her out of here."

Erin was still trying to understand the words she'd heard spoken directly into her ear.

Use what you have. Try.

What did she have? No weapons. Nothing. Not even her purse.

Don't give up. Think.

And then she knew.

She would try.

A female orderly grabbed Erin's arm.

When Erin shook her off, the woman flew over the countertop, smashing into a plant. Where had that come from? God had to be working through her. This was not about who she was, but about who he was.

The burly orderly lunged for Erin. She tossed him into a heap.

Hope held Jenny by the shoulders like a puppy.

"We're not afraid." Barry's jaws clattered.

Then why are they shaking? Erin wondered.

Because you believe. Because you're standing up to them. And because the others are praying.

This wasn't a trick, wasn't something Erin had done on her own power. God was with her. And that was enough.

Erin pulled her keys from her back pocket and threw the pointy hunk of metal like a missile into Demon Girl's forehead. Hope smashed to the ground as Jenny dropped and ran.

Claudia reached for Jenny, leaving Erin to wage the battle God had given her.

Erin turned to Barry. "You're not taking him either." She grabbed a handful of coins from her pocket and fired them like stones from a slingshot. The coins threw sparks as they buried themselves into Barry's tough hide. The beast howled like he was roasting over a spit. He dropped Patch, who dragged Jarrod over to the band of prayer warriors.

GRIM-FACED, THE three stood shoulder to shoulder: The Peaceful One, the Radiant One, and the Shining One. This was their moment.

They formed a rock-hard wall of celestial strength.

Nothing could move them.

58

McCRY LUNGED FOR Patch and Jenny, but something stopped her. It was as though a Plexiglas wall had been erected between her and her prey. She could see the others but she couldn't get through.

She and the two orderlies scratched at the clear screen. Pounding, feeling for an opening. Shoulder to shoulder with McCry the two demons shoved and roared, flapping their wings.

They couldn't make a dent in the barrier.

"No!" she howled at the group of praying teens. "What have you done?" She turned to the orderlies. "Do something!"

SOMEONE MUST STAY.

Patch heard the words in his heart. He refused to listen. Why couldn't they all escape? He would try. What was wrong with that?

Run for the door. Erin will hold them off.

His heart understood before his head.

Patch felt her squeeze his hand. She knew. She let go and turned to face her enemies. McCry and the two orderlies scratched at the clear wall like enraged mimes.

McCry could no longer act like she was in control. Prayer held them all at bay.

But for how long?

Claudia, Nancy, and Granger escaped first. Jarrod stumbled along on his remaining crutch with Jenny. The little girl stopped and looked at Erin. "Please come," she said.

"I'll try," Erin said.

Patch watched. When the breach occurred, she would be standing alone. Waiting. Ready for McCry. Prepared for Hope and Barry.

Their last defense.

Patch wanted to see Jenny safe outside. But he wanted Erin to survive too. Should he run to his small sibling—or try to save his sister in Christ?

Patch looked at Erin.

"It's what God wants." Erin turned toward the devils.

He ran to take care of the others.

ERIN KNEW THEY were still praying, but her strength was waning. She felt God's gift slipping away.

As the demons rose, their strength returned. Erin was her normal self again. The orderly grabbed her around the waist as McCry shouted orders. Erin was trapped.

Patch stood hesitating at the door.

"Go!" she said, as someone punched her.

Erin's hope flickered.

Please rescue me.

PATCH COULDN'T LET it happen again. He had to do something. The thought of watching another friend fall shook him.

But he was not supposed to stay. It wasn't part of the plan.

He had to let her go if that's what God wanted.

"I love you, Erin," he said.

He watched them pull her away. Only a few yards separated them. McCry and her demons turned toward him.

He ran, tears stinging.

Everyone else was in the truck, with Jarrod behind the wheel. Patch jumped into the truck bed, where Granger also crouched.

No other option.

"Keep praying!" Claudia yelled.

The demons burst from the Home and pursued the truck, but an invisible bubble covered it. Demon claws smashed against it and sparks flew, but they couldn't break through. The monsters spat, drooled, and kicked, but the barrier held.

They swept in a huge circle toward the sun. Perhaps preparing for one last attack? *Please God, no!*

Screeching, the failures flew away.

McCRY BURST BACK through the front door, shoving the big orderly. "Why didn't you get the rest of them? I wanted them all."

He yanked Erin's arms behind her back. "Lady, you told us to hold this one."

McCry circled them. "So it takes two of you to keep a child in check? What incompetence!"

Erin almost laughed as McCry tried to reclaim some of her tattered dignity. The woman was ridiculous. "Don't you know God's mercy when it smacks you senseless?" she said. "God rescued them, McCry."

The woman's voice was smooth. "Then why are you here? Not worthy enough?"

"He saved me too," Erin said. "Jesus took away my sins. Yours too."

McCry kneed Erin in the stomach, making her fall.

"Welcome back to your new home, Erin. You will never leave here."

59

"HE GIRL'S NOT worth the trouble," Hope said.

Back to her whining ways, Barry thought. "We can't return empty-handed."

Hope's wings hissed as she screeched back toward the Home.

"What do you have in mind?" Barry coughed on her dust.

"The perfect target." Her voice sounded like clanging metal.

ERIN HEARD THE explosion. Following McCry, another staffer yanking her along, Erin felt so tired. All she wanted was a shower and a minute to think.

McCry came to a stop in front of them. "Look who's back," she said as Barry and Hope swooped in through the hole their claws had torn in the roof. Erin noticed she didn't look happy.

Barry stomped cracks into the tile. Hope grabbed Erin. "You didn't think it would be that easy, did you?" she said.

Was an intelligent conversation with a demon even possible? "Actually, I was praying for a crash landing," Erin said. "And you without your helmet."

Barry dug his claws into her arm. Erin cried out.

"Such wit," he said.

"Pity it will go to waste," McCry said. "I hear the comedy clubs are murder where you're from." She laughed, but Erin saw her eyes darting from demon to demon. She obviously felt out of control, a bully trying to pretend she was brave, which didn't make Erin stop worrying. She was like a scrawny rabbit two wolves wanted for dinner.

"Not a bad line," Hope said to McCry. "The one about the comedy clubs." She looked at Barry and smirked. "How did she know?"

The demons suddenly dropped Erin like a used napkin. They clomped toward McCry. What were they up to?

The woman backed behind the counter, trying to hide. As if.

"Take her," McCry said, pointing at Erin. Still pretending to boss them around.

"Hilarious," Barry said. "You still think you're in charge."

"You think we want that scrawny girl?" Hope said. "I looked better in my costume."

"Humans are so stupid," Barry said. He smashed the desk with his tail, shoved the two pieces apart, and reached for McCry. "But you—you're practically one of us."

"We're all about happiness," Hope said, digging her claws into McCry's forearm. "Your happiness."

Erin covered her mouth.

The woman shrieked. "Help me, Erin! Someone!" No one moved. She cursed the orderlies.

"They won't miss you," Barry said. "Besides, you'll be happier where you're going."

The two smashed through the front door, McCry clutched in Hope's muscled limb, screaming as they took to the sky.

60

Y OU COULDN'T SAVE them both, Patch," Jarrod said. "It was an awful choice, but you had to make it."

Those in the backseat chimed in their agreement, but it didn't make Patch feel any better. "Erin was right. You had to go. She was helping you."

"I'm not worth it. Why'd she do it?"

"Because she loves you," Jarrod said. "But mostly because she loves Jesus."

Jarrod dropped the others off, then drove again to the city park. With McCry gone, the world would be different. Patch hoped things would get better for his friends. Either way, he'd keep praying.

The scene didn't fit what they'd been through. Blue skies, a pond scattered with noisy ducks. Jenny ran through the grass, arms out, twirling herself dizzy. Happiness and pain poured into Patch's soul.

"The offer still stands." Jarrod smiled at Jenny. "She's welcome too."

"You don't know that." Patch refused to give the girl false hope. Jenny hadn't been in the equation when Jarrod made the offer the first time. "You know they're going to come for me again."

"Counting on it."

"But your parents? What would they say to two extra kids around the house?"

"She probably eats like a hummingbird."

Jenny flapped her arms, the breeze swirling her hair.

Jarrod held out his cell phone. "Ask them yourself."

"Hey, man. I really appreciate it. But . . . before I do anything, I'd like to take a walk, think things through. Can you watch Jenny for me?"

With his sister safe with Jarrod, Patch took off walking, wandering aimlessly. He couldn't believe what had just happened. To finally return to his friends. Finally return to Erin. And then lose her again. For good, this time, he was sure. His heart ached.

Against his will—or perhaps because of it—his feet took him toward the Home. He knew it wasn't safe, but something compelled him. He needed to know for sure that Erin was gone.

He walked, praying, until the Home came into sight. It was a mess. Plate glass shattered all over the front lawn, people milling around.

He stood, looking through the gaping holes in the front of the building. Inside he could see someone picking her way through the rubble. A young woman—a girl. Slim, with long hair. Sunlight hit her face . . .

Patch took off toward the door at a run. When he reached the opening, he stopped. Inside, the girl moved through the debris. When she heard him, she looked up, smiled, and ran to him.

Patch and Erin embraced, laughing and crying. When they finally broke apart, Patch looked at her in disbelief.

"God wanted me to trust him enough to give you up," he said.

"Thanks a lot." But she grinned. He hugged her again.

Several of the hospital staff looked at them warily. Patch figured they'd start asking questions soon. He'd rather not be there for that. "Guess we should leave."

"For now. I want to visit these kids again." Erin took Patch's hand.

61

PATCH HATED TO drop Erin off at her home, but she insisted. "I've got to work things out. And I miss Terry. We can talk later."

"I understand." He pulled Jenny close. The three stood outside the Morgan house. They huddled together, saying good-bye while Jarrod waited in the truck. "But I'll be back for you."

Hesitating, he reached into his pocket and handed Erin something. A shiny ring.

"That's not—" Erin said.

Patch folded her fingers around the jewelry. "Nope. Just something I've been meaning to give you for a long time." He had a hard time swallowing for the emotion in his heart.

She slipped on the friendship token, planted a kiss on his cheek, and then ran into the house. As she shut the door, he heard Terry calling her name.

Heaving a sigh, Patch hugged Jenny. He knew Erin would have a tough time. But he also had seen God work miracles.

"Come on, kiddo. Let's go."

They climbed into the car. Jarrod smiled but said nothing. He held out his cell and started the car.

Patch took the phone. "Hello?"

"You get yourself back here, son. And bring that little girl with you." Jarrod's mother sounded like she wouldn't take no for an answer. So he didn't say it.

"Yes, ma'am."

"Well, then, that's settled. We'll see you when you get here. Take care of yourself."

"Yes, ma'am."

Jarrod grinned as Patch ended the call. He put the truck in gear and drove the clanking vehicle down the street, slow and steady. No hurry, no worry.

"You didn't think my parents could resist her, did you?" Jarrod said, gesturing at Jenny, who had curled up against Patch and closed her eyes.

"Impossible."

Patch smiled and closed his own eyes in a prayer of thanks. He was leaving loved ones. But he was also going toward loved ones. With his sister and his brother in Christ at his side.

He was part of a family again.

About the Authors

 **JERRY B. JENKINS** is the author of more than 170 books, including fifteen *New York Times* bestsellers. He is the author (with Tim LaHaye) of the multi-million selling Left Behind series. His Left Behind, the Kids series, coauthored with Chris Fabry, sold more than 10 million books. He and his wife have three grown sons and four grandchildren.

 **JOHN PERRODIN** is a novelist, researcher, speaker, and attorney. He serves as Senior Editor for the Jerry B. Jenkins Christian Writers Guild. John and his wife, Sue, have been married for more than twenty years and have seven children.